Amanda

A Needful Bride

Danni Roan

Copyright © 2020 Danni Roan

All rights reserved

The characters and events portrayed in this book are fictitious. Any similarity to real persons, living or dead, is coincidental and not intended by the author.

No part of this book may be reproduced, or stored in a retrieval system, or transmitted in any form or by any means, electronic, mechanical, photocopying, recording, or otherwise, without express written permission of the publisher.

ISBN: 9798681112051
Cover design by: Erin Dameron-Hill
Library of Congress Control Number: 2018675309
Printed in the United States of America

Contents

Title Page
Copyright
Introduction

Chapter 1	1
Chapter 2	9
Chapter 3	26
Chapter 4	37
Chapter 5	54
Chapter 6	75
Chapter 7	92
Chapter 8	109
Chapter 9	115
Chapter 10	126
Chapter 11	137
Chapter 12	148
Chapter 13	157

Chapter 14	164
Chapter 15	178
Chapter 16	185
Epilogue	200
Books In This Series	207

Introduction

Teddy Lewis has waited long enough to receive his mail-order bride, but she is nowhere to be seen. As impatience mounts, the young cowman doesn't let an opportunity go to waste when an emergency calls Olive Hampton away, leaving the newest arrival in Needful, Texas entirely on her own.

Amanda Antonia has lost everything she ever owned and loved when her mother remarries, scandalously soon, after the death of Amanda's father. Seeking a new start in life and a loving protector of her own, she is soon tossed into the wilds of Texas, utterly unprepared for rowdy cowboys, roaming cattle, and riotous romance.

Chapter 1

"Olive! Olive Hampton!" Teddy Lewis came charging into the small town of Needful, Texas, bellowing at the top of his lungs, mere seconds behind the stagecoach from Colbert's Ferry.

"Olive!" The young puncher hit the ground before his black and white pinto had come to a stop at the front of the hitching rail. Stomping onto the porch, Teddy bellowed again, "Olive!"

"Lands sakes," Olive Hampton opened the door, her dark eyes sharp. "What on earth is the matter with you, Teddy?" The aged, yet slender boardinghouse keeper asked, drying her hands on a dishtowel.

"Daliah sent me for you. She says she needs you to come to the ranch. Pete's horse fell on him, and she needs you to help set his shoulder. It's hangin' like a broke limb in a winter storm."

The young man let his arm dangle at his side as

if it were no longer attached to his body in a grotesque parody of the real injury.

A soft gasp made Olive and Teddy turn as a young woman in a dusty white dress stepped off the stage, her pale blue eyes wide with repulsion.

"I'll fetch my things," Olive said. "Orville will be around with fresh horses for the stage, and then he'll bring me to the ranch."

"Are you Mrs. Hampton?" the petite dark-haired young woman stepped daintily toward the pair. "I'm Amanda Antonia."

"Good heavens," Olive sighed. "I'm afraid you've arrived at an inopportune time. If you'll go into the boarding house and let one of my daughters-in-law know who you are, they'll fix everything up. I'm afraid I'm needed elsewhere. Excuse me."

The sound of galloping horses and the crack of a pistol shot rang out across the town, making the young woman scream and crumple toward the boardwalk.

Teddy leapt, his strong arms catching the slight form of the pretty woman before she crashed to the hard planks of the boardinghouse front stoop. Her face was pale, her eyes closed, and her body trembled in his hands.

"Now what?" Olive snapped, spinning and seeing the prone young woman. "Oh my!"

"You go on, Olive." Teddy scooped the girl into his arms. "I'll see to this one. Daliah said she needed you something terrible. Said no one else could understand what she was tellin' them to do."

Olive looked between the cowhand and the corner of the boarding house where her husband was bringing a fresh team of horses for the stage. "I'll be back as soon as I can. One of the girls will help you with our new arrival." She shook her head once, then hefted her long skirts and stepped into the street headed for the livery as she called to her husband.

***

"Miss, Miss." Teddy's voice was soft as he gazed into the lovely face before him, but the young woman was beyond hearing. She was out in a dead faint, possibly brought on by the rowdy cowboys whooping their way through town. "Now, don't you worry none," Teddy drawled. "Ol' Teddy will look after you."

The sound of a buckboard racing away from the livery told Teddy that Olive and Orville were on their way to the ranch, even as the livery hand, Darwin, came to help change horses for the stage.

Theodore Lewis was on his own to care for the

new, probable, Needful bride. Teddy had placed an order for a bride with Olive several months ago, but so far, it seemed that every time a new woman arrived in Needful, another lucky man snatched her up before Teddy had a chance to say howdy-do. A bright glint sparkled in the young man's eyes, and looking around him, an idea was born.

Down the street, Theodore Lewis could hear the sheriff shouting at the overly enthusiastic cowboys who had startled this delicate flower, and the stage, now equipped with fresh horses, was headed out of town.

Lifting the slight form in his arms, Teddy hurried to his pony, slipping a boot into a stirrup and tossing his burden over the saddle swells. Adjusting his seat so that the young woman's head rested against his breast, he snatched up the bridle reins and laid spurs to his painted horse, dusting it out of town before anyone else could see him with his prize.

***

Teddy didn't slow until he was close enough to the ranch to see the outbuildings, then he eased his heaving mount to a slow walk, turning toward the old pools and the tiny cabin he had built over the past few months in his spare time. The place wasn't much, but with a woman's touch, he was convinced the little place would make a fine home.

Teddy had arrived in Texas with his former commander, Dan Gaines, now Mayor of Needful, and had made the place his home. War-weary and jaded by all that he had seen, the young man, though youthful in appearance, was old of soul.

Teddy wanted nothing more than a few head of cattle, a decent horse under him, and someone to love. So far, Olive and Peri, the local matchmakers, had failed to bring him the desire of his heart, but today the Good Lord had seen fit to lay her right in his lap. Maybe he wasn't the best cowpuncher, the brightest mind, or the best looking man in Needful, but Teddy knew he would make a wonderful husband and provider if given half the chance.

Flicking his dark eyes to the light burden resting across his knees, Teddy smiled. "You wait and see," he said. "You'll find I'm just what you were lookin' for here in Needful. I have a lot of love to give, a nice little place, and faith that everything will be alright in the end."

***

"Did you ever see someone put up such a fuss?" Olive sighed, stumbling into the boarding house, hours later, through the back door with Orville on her heels.

"Now, Olive, Pete was in a good deal of pain,"

the tall old man with the shock of white hair ran a hand over his face.

"I'm not talking about Pete," Olive snapped. "I'm talking about the other men that were there to help put his shoulder back. They cringed like mice, every time we told them to hold Pete, that arm would have been set much sooner if everyone wouldn't have worried so about hurting the man."

"Well, Pete is their friend." Orville's voice was reasonable, but Olive still shot him a stern look.

"A moment of pain to set things right is better than suffering for weeks. It's a good thing you men aren't the ones having babies," she added with a grin. "The human race would disappear."

Orville chuckled, spinning Olive toward him as he grasped her hand and kissing her on the lips. "You're a wonder, Olive Hampton," he grinned, heading to the kitchen to wash up. "I hope supper's ready. I'm starved."

"Arabela?" Olive walked toward the outer kitchen, looking for her daughter-in-law. "Girls, where are you? What have you done with Amanda?"

"Hello, Mother Hampton," the tall, black-haired beauty greeted. "Who is Amanda?"

"The new bride who arrived on the stage today,"

Olive said, peering into the dining room of the boarding house. "I told her to come to one of you girls, and you'd get her settled. Teddy was there when she arrived."

"We have no new guests." Arabela raised a brow. The woman could appear cold at first glance but was a good and loving wife to her husband and family.

"Guests?" Ellen Hampton walked into the kitchen, an empty serving tray in her hands, and looked questioningly at her mother-in-law. "We don't have any new guests. The stage delivered the mail and was gone."

"I was on the porch when the girl stepped off the stage," Olive grumbled. "I saw her with my own two eyes. She can't have simply disappeared."

"She didn't come in here." Ellen slipped her long blonde braid over her shoulder. "You don't think she wandered off, do you? It's still barely safe for a decent woman to walk through town on her own. Why just this morning, Sheriff Gaines arrested a group of cowboys for shooting their way through Needful."

"I'll check the rooms," Olive offered wearily, "you send one of the children to the sawmill and ask my sons if they've seen a stranger." The older woman tapped her lip with her index finger. "I'll send for the preacher as well."

"The preacher?" Shililaih, Olive's third daughter-in-law, stepped into the now crowded kitchen, a pitcher in hand. "Why do we need the preacher?" the pretty strawberry-blonde grinned. "Who's getting' married?"

"Olive lost a bride," Arbela's face was passive, but her blue eyes sparkled with delight. "She swears a young woman got off the stage, but none of us have seen her."

"What if she was kidnapped?" Shililaih asked excitedly. "Do you want me to fetch Sheriff Spencer?"

"Shi, don't be dramatic, "Olive scolded, running a hand over weary eyes. "The girl has probably just wandered off." Her face grew still as her eyes widened. "No, I don't think so." Olive's dark eyes sparked with realization. "I remember now. Teddy Lewis rode in to tell me Daliah needed my help at the ranch. Amanda, that's the girl's name," she snapped her fingers. "She fainted when those cowboys came whooping through town. Teddy said he'd take care of her."

"Then where is she?" Ellen sighed, shaking her head.

"Exactly!"

Chapter 2

Amanda opened her eyes, blinking to bring the room into focus. She had been shot, with an anguished cry she sat bolt upright running her hands over her body to find the bullet hole.

"Easy there now," a warm, rich voice washed over her, and Amanda looked up into a man's strong, handsome, and youthful face.

"I've been shot!" she screeched.

"No, no, you're all right. You ain't been shot. It was just some rowdy cowboys havin' some fun." The man smiled, flashing even, white teeth as he knelt before her. "I'm Teddy," he grinned. "Teddy Lewis."

Amanda felt her heart rate begin to slow as she clutched her middle, feeling the nervous jitter in her stomach. "Where am I?"

"You're safe."

Amanda relaxed a bit at the man's words. He

seemed a nice sort of fellow, though dusty and rather rugged in attire.

"I was supposed to meet Olive Hampton." Amanda looked around her again, this time, her brain taking in the simple hut around her. She was sitting on a bench covered in cowhide with the hair still on. "Is this the boarding house?" She looked down into the man's face as he squatted before her.

"No, no. Not exactly," Teddy rose to his feet, abruptly pacing to a fireplace and pouring a cup of coffee. "Here, you drink this. It'll make you feel better."

Amanda reached up, taking the tin cup from his hand, a questioning look in her eyes. "If this isn't the boarding house," she asked, taking a sip of the bitter brew, "where am I?"

Teddy licked his lips, pacing to the door, which stood open, letting in a soft breeze. "Well," he began, shoving his hands in his back pockets. "You see, when you fainted, I was worried for ya, and so…" he turned, meeting her pale eyes. "Ya, see… I kinda brought you home."

"Home?" Amanda's eyes grew wide as she gazed around her at the four walls and simple appointments. "Whose home?"

"Mine."

AMANDA

Amanda's hands began to shake, the coffee threatening to spill over onto her dust-bedraggled dress as tears filled her eyes.

"You brought me to your house," her voice quivered. "How could you? I'm a single woman alone with a man I've never met before. What will everyone think?" A bright tear splashed onto her cheek and Teddy's heart cracked.

"It ain't like that," he pleaded, running his hands through his light brown hair. "I mean, I know we're alone, but the door has been open this whole time."

"And who knows I'm here?" Amanda asked. "What, what are your intentions?"

"My intentions?" Teddy's eyes grew wide. "My intentions are honorable. I assure you. I'd never hurt a woman. I just. Well, I just wanted…"

"You wanted what?" Amanda's stomach turned over with fear. Why had this strange man brought her to his home instead of taking her into the boarding house where she would have been safe? What was he playing at?

"I just wanted a chance to meet you is all."

"Meet me!" Amanda's voice was shrill. "You kidnapped me. What kind of man are you? I came here to be a bride and some crazy cowboy kidnaps me."

"It's ain't like that," Teddy raised his hands as if in surrender. "See, Olive promised me a bride, but every time a new girl comes to town she's married before I hardly even knew it. I just wanted a couple of minutes alone with you, so you'd know who I am."

Amanda's breath caught in her throat as her eyes met his. He seemed so sincere, yet his behavior was beyond inappropriate.

"I'm sorry for your troubles," she said, standing on shaky legs, "but what you did was wrong. You've put me in a terrible situation. What man is going to want me knowing I've spent an afternoon in your accommodations, completely alone?" Fresh tears spilled over, dampening her cheeks, and Amanda felt her hopes evaporate in the hot Texas sun. "I'm ruined."

"No, no, you ain't." Teddy stepped up, placing his hands on her shoulders, removing them quickly when she cringed. "I guess I wasn't thinkin'," he admitted. "I just saw a chance and took it. There you were, pretty as a picture, the most lovely girl I ever did see, and you was alone and helpless. I figured it wouldn't hurt if I brought you to the ranch for a minute, so's we could get to know each other."

"Well, it was wrong of you," Amanda sniffed, wringing her delicate hands. "I'm leaving." She shuffled toward the door keeping an eye on the young man to see if he would try to stop her. Emboldened by his look of chagrin, Amanda slipped through the door and out into the bright sunlight of a late summer's day.

Gazing around her, Amanda spotted a well-worn trail and stepped out boldly, hoping it would lead her back to town and the safety of the Hampton's lodging.

Teddy studied the tips of his scuffed boots for several seconds, his thoughts muddled as the implications of what he had done struck home. He hadn't meant to cause problems for the newly arrived young woman. He had wanted to meet her was all. What harm was there in bringing her here? All the ranch hands were respectable, or at least well behaved after Dan Gaines had laid down the law to them.

Everyone knew Teddy Lewis to be a hard-working, upstanding member of Needful, Texas, a dependable, law-abiding, and God-fearing young man. No one would think the worst of him having Miss Amanda in his home.

Teddy scratched his head, pondering the issue. It looked like his bright idea had not gone to plan. Instead of impressing the young woman, he had frightened her away.

Everything seemed to snap into focus as Teddy's head jerked up. Where had she gone? He had thought she had simply stepped out onto the tiny porch of his cabin, but now she was nowhere to be seen. Snatching his hat from its peg, Teddy smashed it onto his head and strode out into the open prairie around him.

"Miss Amanda," he called, looking toward the ranch, then down the old cattle trail, as his heart stuttered. A flash of white fluttered on the breeze dropping behind the hill that led to the pools below.

Sprinting down the trail, Teddy's heart began to pound. The pretty little thing he had brought home was headed straight into danger.

"Wait! Wait!" he cried, topping the rise, as a scream echoed into the heat of the day.

Teddy raced down the hill as a huge bull stepped into the path, separating him from the young woman in the white dress, and his blood ran cold.

"Hey, bull!" Teddy bellowed, waving his arms at the massive black and white creature that swung his head of deadly horns toward Teddy. "Hey, hey!" the cowboy yelled, taking off his hat and waving it.

With a snort, the longhorn swung toward him, lowering its head and pawing the ground.

Teddy felt the sweat bead on his neck and his eyes flickered toward the trees willing the young woman to hide among them, even as the bull charged.

Two tons of angry beef charging toward him sent Teddy's senses into overdrive, and he dodged away as the beast skidded past, sliding to a stop and wheeling for another run at the trim cowhand.

Teddy waved his hat, trying to distract the bull who bellowed at him in rage as it tore up the earth and charged again.

This time the bull clipped the hat from Teddy's hand, snagging it on an upturned span of a shimmering, steel-like horn. Turning again, the bull shook its head, eyes rolling, as it tried to shake the impaled hat from where it dangled, but the item stuck fast.

"Miss Amanda, hide in them trees," Teddy called, keeping his eyes pinned on the bull. "Get in the narrows where he can't reach ya."

A squeak behind him told Teddy that the girl had complied.

The bull bellowed again, foam and snot dripping from its nostrils as it charged once more.

Teddy risked a glance behind him, seeing a shimmer of white between the thick clump of trees. The pounding of hooves echoed behind him and Teddy broke into a run. If he made it to the trees, he could outwait the enraged bull. His boots thudded on the hard-packed earth. As Teddy sprinted, he could feel the immense power of the beast behind him as it gained momentum. His hands reached out, grasping a sapling and spinning into the thicket as something sharp grazed his back pockets, and he yelped in pain.

Teddy stumbled into the thicket, his hands grabbing his posterior as he tumbled to the ground between two heavy trees, biting his lip against the pain.

"Are you okay?" he asked, panting as his backside burned.

The young woman took one look at the prostrate man then looked up as the bull attacked a small tree, shredding the limbs to splinters and dropped to the earth in a dead faint.

Teddy sprang to his feet with a hiss of pain and gathered the woman into his arms, pulling her back into the heart of the clump of trees as the bull huffed and paced outside.

An eternity later, the soft lowing of cows was a

sweet sound to his ears as Teddy watched the rest of the herd meander toward the pools on the other side of the trees. A rangy red and white cow lifted her head, bellowing as the rest of the stock fell in behind her on the trek to water.

With a final shake of his head, the big bull turned back toward the rest of the cattle, Teddy's hat still dangling from one glimmering horn.

***

"Teddy?" Dan Gaines rode over the top of the rise, pulling his horse to a stop as his friend and fellow wrangler staggered toward him, cringing with every step. "What you got there?" the other man asked, a grin playing about his lips.

"This here is Miss Amanda," Teddy shifted the unconscious woman in his arms. "We had a bit of trouble with a bull."

Dan Gaines sat up straight in the saddle, his blue eyes glinting with concern. "Is she injured?"

"No, she passed out. I, on the other hand, may require a few days off and a new pair of trousers." He turned slightly, exposing his torn pants and the blood-stained flesh beneath.

Dan pushed his hat back on his head of brown hair, this time, the grin flashing to life. "You did make a mess of things, didn't you, Theodore?"

"Just give me a hand," Teddy growled, handing the prostrate woman up to his boss. "We'll get her back to the ranch."

"You'd best get to the cabin and change," Dan nodded. "You have company waiting up at the ranch. Rosa hasn't stopped laughing since Olive and Orville arrived."

Teddy swallowed hard but nodded, finally finding his voice. "Is Spence with 'em?"

"No," Dan adjusted the pretty young thing in his arms. She looked far too delicate for a rowdy cow town in Texas, and he wondered what her story was. "I'll get her back to the ranch while you change. I don't think this is a case for the law, but you have a lot of explaining to do."

Teddy nodded, his face flushing red. "I'll be along."

Dan pinned him with his eyes one more time, but the smile remained. "Confound it, Ted, where's your hat?"

***

Teddy slammed his old cavalry cap onto his head and trudged gingerly to the main house of the Double D ranch. He could see the buckboard from where he was, and for a moment, he wished that old bull had finished him off. He hadn't meant any harm bringing Miss Amanda to his place. He was just tired of being alone. With his long days in the saddle and few trips to town, he had all but given up on the hope of a new bride coming to Needful. So far, every time a girl turned up in the town, she was married off before he'd had a chance to say howdy.

Teddy shook his head at his predicament. He had spoken to Olive on several occasions, and she had assured him that the right girl would be along, but when? He'd be an old man by the time the boardinghouse keeper and town matchmaker got around to finding him a bride.

Swiping the cap from his head, he sighed. It had seemed like a good idea at the time to bring the young woman to the ranch, but in hindsight, maybe he should have taken her to the Hampton women. Look at the mess he was in now. Miss Amanda would never give him the time of day, now that she thought he had kidnapped her. On top of that, he'd not be sittin' a saddle for several days, and the Captain was bound to have a few words on that count.

Teddy shook his head again, shoving the cap over his dark locks. No, Dan was not a Captain anymore, and Teddy was his own free man. After the war, he had chosen to follow Gaines and his loyal crew to Texas, where they had built something, gathering a herd from the wild cattle that lived on the plains.

He was a free man with a free will, and he wasn't going to give up so easily on the pretty girl he had just saved from certain death.

Tugging his shirt straight, Teddy pulled the cap down low, squared his shoulders and stepped up onto the porch of the main house. It was time to face the music, but he knew how to dance. One way or another, he would prove to Miss Amanda that he was the right man for her and that she would be safe with him.

Teddy was sick of being alone with his own demons. He was tired of feeling like he'd wandered the face of the earth, through hell and high water, for nothing. Theodore Lewis was going to make his life mean something.

***

"Dan, what are you going to do about this situation?" Olive's voice was the first thing Teddy heard as he stepped through the door. "That girl could have been killed."

"It ain't Captain, I mean Mayor Dan's fault," Teddy said, his voice firm. "I did what I did for my own reasons."

"Theodore Lewis," Olive spun, pointing a finger in his face. "What on earth were you thinking?"

"I was thinking that maybe this time, I'd get a chance to introduce myself to a young woman what had come here to marry." Teddy's eyes flashed.

Olive withdrew her finger, looking to Orville for support.

"I know you can't always control what happens when these girls arrive," Teddy continued. "I was just tired of waiting, and when Miss Amanda all but dropped into my lap, I took my chance. For all I know, she hates me for it, and maybe my head was all muddled by a pretty face and all, but that's what it is."

"Teddy, why don't you have a seat?" Dan asked, that smile teasing his lips again. "Rosa, would you get Ted some coffee, please?" Dan turned, his bright eyes softening as he looked at his petite black-haired wife.

"Si," Rosa smiled. "I will get more coffee." The petite woman winked at Teddy. "You want a pillow to sit?"

Teddy could feel his face heating as he shook his head. "Where's Miss Amanda?" he asked, his voice soft. "I'd like to apologize."

"I'm glad to see you survived," Amanda walked into the room from the parlor, waving Dan away as he stood. "I'm afraid I've had quite a fright today."

Teddy nodded, looking the young woman up and down to assess if she had been injured. Her pretty dress was dirty, her hair half down, and her eyes wide with bewilderment.

"I'm sorry for any part I played in your discomfort, ma'am," he drawled. "It was not my intention to upset you." Slowly Teddy twisted his hat in his hands as his heart twisted in the wind. "I hope that in time you'll be able to forgive me for my rash behavior. If you ever need anything, all you need to do is ask."

Amanda looked up, meeting the young man's dark gaze. He was such a good looking young man, his youthful appearance belying his ancient eyes. There was more to this man than one could comprehend at first glance, but his behavior had been beyond appalling.

"I'd like to go back to town," Amanda said, tearing her eyes from Teddy's. "Mr. Lewis." She walked to Olive, taking the older woman's arm.

Rosa returned, handing Teddy his coffee. "You drink," she said, her deep brown eyes full of laughter. "All will be well, you see."

Teddy shook his head as Amanda, Olive, and Orville walked out the front door. He had been a fool, and his last chance at happiness seemed to leave with them.

"I'm sorry." His words drifted after the trio through the open door on the wings of a prayer.

Dan slapped Teddy on the back with a hearty chuckle, making the younger man cringe. "I don't know what got into you," he laughed. "I've never known you to do anything so foolish before."

Teddy shrugged, his mind racing back to a few times in his life where he had thrown caution to the wind and risked it all.

"That ain't true," an older man walked in through the front door, his sleepy eyes belying the intelligence beneath. "I recollect a time he sneaked into the enemy camp like a thief to reconnoiter. Counted every man jack in the group and reported back what he'd seen."

Dan's eyes flickered toward Teddy. As the youngest wrangler on his ranch, he felt somewhat responsible for Teddy. Though the man before him swore he had been sixteen when he signed on with the Union, Dan had always had his doubts. How old was he now? Twenty? Twenty-two?

"There's no accounting for the foolishness of youth," Dan grinned.

"You men, always boasting." Rosa shook her head, placing her hands on hips. "Teddy, you were foolish." Her statement was blunt, but the young man didn't argue. "You like this girl?"

"Yes, ma'am," Teddy agreed. "I do."

"Then you will need to show her you do not give up. Give it time then we will go visit."

"Mama," a little dark-haired girl toddled toward Rosa making her grin. "I hungry."

"Now," Rosa looked around the room. "We eat."

Dan scooped up the little girl, snuggling her close. He loved Rosa's daughter and vowed daily to do his best to raise her as her late father, Raul, would have wanted. Still newlywed, Dan was adjusting to life with the fiery woman he loved. He would never have dreamed his life would have taken this turn, but his heart was grateful that it did.

Dan had met Raul, a top hand and trader from Mexico, almost three years earlier, and when the man had been killed in a misguided raid across the border, Dan had felt responsible.

Christina patted his face and giggled as the stubble on his chin, tickled her hands. It had taken a good deal of time, and a lot of prayer to set the past behind and accept the love he had for Rosa and her daughter. Dan, an honorable man, had resisted the truth right up until the moment he had rescued Rosa from a group of very bad men.

"I hope you won't mind if I stand to eat my supper," Teddy offered with a blush looking around as the other men laughed. "I guess Dan told you what happened."

Dozer slapped Teddy on the shoulder, ushering them into the large room on the side of the house where they took their meals. "I reckon you'll be on barn duty for the week," the older man chuckled. "Just be glad nothing important was injured."

Chapter 3

Teddy pushed the broom over the outer porch of the big ranch house. He'd been put on barn duty and was now helping Rosa with chores and maintenance around the house, anything that didn't require him to sit.

"Don't see why I couldn't keep her," the young man grumbled to the empty sky. "Didn't she come here to get married?" The sting in his backside from nearly being killed by an angry bull rankled far less than the fact that he'd barely had a minute to talk to pretty Amanda.

"You talkin' to yourself again?" Cookie trundled out of the house, taking a seat on one of the rocking chairs there. "Seem's that old bull didn't help your disposition none," the old man chortled.

"It ain't that ol' bull that has me piqued."

"Only thing can work a man up like this is a woman." Cookie looked up from his chair, his eyes twinkling.

"Women," Teddy spat. "They all seem to want to keep me in the dark forever. Just 'cause I'm the youngest fella here don't mean I shouldn't be allowed to find a wife. I ordered a bride from Olive ages ago, and the minute I get a chance to meet one of these young women, they call me every kind of a fool."

"Well, maybe you need to stop actin' like a fool and start to courtin' that girl proper like?"

Teddy turned, squinting at the old man. "What are you on about, Cookie?" he asked. "Spill the beans."

Cookie leaned forward, meeting the young man's eyes. "You need to get slicked up and go to town. Bring a passel of posies, maybe buy somethin' pretty and go see that girl."

Teddy's hand edged toward his damaged derriere. "I still can't sit a horse," he growled. "Probably some other fella already scooped up that pretty Amanda."

Cookie leaned back with a grin, setting his rocker in motion once more. "Seems to me I need to get to town," the old man sighed. "I reckon, what with my rheumatism someone else best hitch the team and ride along with me."

A slow smile crept across Teddy's face as he eyed the old ranch cook. "A nice quiet ride to town would be a nice change from things round here," he drawled. "I'll hitch the team."

***

"Where's the new girl?" Periwinkle Cassidy strode into the boarding house, gazing around her for any glimpse of a new face.

"Perwe," her mother's slurred words trailed her and she cringed.

"Sorry, Mama," Peri sighed. "I just want to meet her and find out what all the gossip is about."

"Mrs. Perkins, would you like some tea?" Jacks Verone asked, escorting the older woman to a chair, his kind eyes keen.

"'ess," Mercy Perkins hissed, offering a crooked smile to her escort.

Jacks had generously offered to bring Mercy and her daughter to town when Peri's husband Bear, Bartholomew, had been roped into helping her other son-in-law, Anderson, with some work on his prosperous cattle ranch.

"Mama, I'm going to find Olive," Peri smiled as Jacks helped her mother to a chair. "I'll be out to join you shortly."

"You go on, Peri," Jacks offered. "I'll keep your mother company."

"Seems you been doing that a lot," Peri mumbled under her breath, ducking through the door that separated the family living quarters from the boardinghouse proper.

"Excuse me?" Jacks asked.

"Oh, nothing!" Peri piped, hurrying out of sight. "Olive, are you here?"

"Peri, is that you?" Olive hurried into the hall with a smile for her young friend. Peri's blue eyes sparkled as she pulled off her bonnet, revealing dark blonde hair. "What are you doing here?"

"I came to meet the new bride," Peri replied simply. "I hear she had a bit of an adventure and thought we might want to find out a little about her to determine who she might be suited to."

Olive rolled her eyes, giving a shake of her head. "I can't believe that Teddy took her back to his place," she sighed. "What got into that man's head, I don't know. You'd think he would have a little patience and understand that we'll match him with the right woman at the right time."

Peri chuckled, following Olive toward the main living quarters. "I know that's how it's supposed to work," she grinned, "but so far every time a new bride arrives and we have it all figured out with who to match her with, she ends up with someone else."

Olive shot a knowing look back at Peri. "I'm afraid that's true. Why I was sure your sister, Primrose, was perfect for Dan Gaines, but that didn't go to plan at all."

"Nor with Beth, or Ruth, either. Who would have thought that Mayor Dan carried a torch for Rosa?" Peri giggled.

"I sure didn't see it. Have a seat," Olive added headed for the tea kettle on the hob. "Did you come into town on your own today?"

"No, Jacks brought Mother and me." Peri's eyes twinkled at the mention of the two older people who seemed to have bonded over her mother's ill health.

"How is your mother?" Olive continued getting a teapot from a shelf. "She was much improved the last time I saw her in church."

"Mother's doing well," Peri admitted. "I thought she'd never get better after her stroke, but being here in Texas seems to agree with her."

Olive scooped loose tea into the pot then poured the hot water over them, replacing the lid, as she turned to retrieve cups. "Is she still speaking?"

"It's a struggle, but she gets her point across. She still hums a good deal, and Prim says she loves the

AMANDA

rocking chair Bear made her. She sits, rocks, and hums."

"I'll go out and see her shortly," Olive said, placing the tea things on the table. "First, let's put our heads together about Amanda and what to do about her. She's still rather upset about what happened."

"Why ever for?" Peri asked. "From what I hear, Teddy was a perfect gentleman and even saved her from a fearsome beast. It's not like she spent the night in a strange man's bed," she added with a blush.

"I haven't pressed her too much," Olive admitted pouring the tea and offering a cup to Peri. "Amanda seems a bit delicate if you ask me."

"Delicate!" Peri's blue eyes grew wide over the rim of her cup. "She isn't sickly, is she?"

"I don't think so." Olive shook her head. "She doesn't seem suited to life here in Texas, though. Perhaps if we could find her a quiet storekeeper, or someone with means who could coddle her a bit, she would be all right."

Peri lowered her cup to the table, meeting Olive's dark eyes. "You'd better send for her. I'd like to meet her, and we can do an interview. Maybe that will point us in the right direction. Besides, I don't know of anyone in town that meets the requirements you mentioned."

"Oh, hello, Peri," Ellen smiled as she walked into the small, family kitchen. "I saw your mother in the dining room and thought you might be about."

"Ellen, would you mind asking Miss Antonia to join us? Peri would like to meet her." Olive smiled at her pretty daughter-in-law. It had been a big surprise when the rest of the Hampton family had joined them just before the first snowfall last year, but Olive was glad her boys and their families had moved to Needful.

"Of course," Ellen grinned. "I see you two are already plotting what comes next for Amanda." Ellen paused for a moment. "That girl sure has some pretty things," she added with a sigh.

Peri looked at Olive, who only shrugged as Ellen left the room.

"You asked to see me," Amanda appeared in the kitchen a few minutes later. "Oh, hello." She turned, greeting Peri. "I'm Amanda Antonia," she offered her lace-covered hand.

"Pleased to meet you, I'm Peri." Peri grinned.

"Amanda, won't you join us?" Olive indicated the tea set. "Peri is my partner in the matchmaking business, and I wanted you to get acquainted."

Peri studied the young woman with critical eyes. She was dressed in one of the airiest dresses the girl from Tennessee had ever seen. It was very expensive and exquisitely made, fitting the small woman's slim waist and delicate curves with precision.

"Your dress is lovely," Peri said as Amanda took a seat. "Where are you from?"

"Virginia," Amanda took a seat, carefully smoothing the skirt of her pale pink dress. The color complimented the young woman's pale complexion and brown hair. "Are you from here?"

"I am now," Peri grinned. "I came here to find out if my sister had found the love of her life and met my own." A soft laugh tittered from Peri, making the other woman smile.

Amanda picked up the cup and saucer, lifting it carefully and sipping. "What do I do now?" she asked, placing the cup back on the table. "I'm afraid I'm rather lost after what happened. Surely no decent man will want me after that Teddy fellow took me to his home."

Peri reached out, patting the girl's hand. She seemed very young, though her letter had indicated she was nineteen. "Just tell us a little about yourself."

Amanda blinked between the two other

women, surprised when neither of them seemed at all concerned about her day alone with the cowhand.

"I'm from Virginia." She stopped looking for a response and then continued when no one else spoke. "I'm the oldest of three children but the only daughter." Amanda swallowed, lifting her cup once more. "My mother recently remarried," she spoke over the rim. "I. I didn't get along with my step-father."

"So you came to Needful to be a bride," Peri nodded with understanding, her green eyes shining with excitement. "I'm sure it's difficult having your father replaced."

Amanda blushed a bit but didn't reply. There were some things she didn't care to share with strangers. "What will happen to me now?" she blurted. "Who will be willing to marry me if they think I'm a ruined woman?"

"Ruined?" Olive gasped. "No one will think that I assure you. Why Teddy might be rash, but he would never take advantage of a woman."

Amanda placed her cup back on the table with trembling hands. "I can't go back home," she sniffed, pulling a hanky from her sleeve. "I can't abide my step-father and would be shamed if I did."

AMANDA

"Don't you worry, dear," Olive smiled. "We'll find you the perfect match. That's what Peri and I do." The older woman squirmed slightly in her chair at the half-truth. They did try to match couples appropriately, but things never seemed to go to plan.

Olive's words seemed to have the desired effect on the girl, and she straightened with a smile. "Thank you. I'm putting myself in your hands."

"Now, tell us what you like to do." Peri smiled encouragingly. "Do you sew? Are you a good cook? Perhaps you can ride well."

Amanda's eyes grew wide with each question. She was very good with cross stitch and needlepoint but had never tried her hand at a garment. She had always had people for that. "I don't cook. I do ride, though."

"Well, that's good," Peri grinned. "I know I enjoy riding, though I'm not much good at it. You just wait and see, we'll find you the perfect mate. Needful is brimming with men looking for a wife."

Olive looked at Peri, a worried expression on her face. This girl didn't seem to know how to do any of the basics a wife in Needful would require. How were they supposed to find a match from the men of the town for a delicate flower like this? At least the other girls had a bit of pluck even if they weren't skilled in the homemaking arts, while this girl seemed shy at best.

"What did you say your family did?" Olive asked.

"I'm afraid I didn't," Amanda admitted. "Is it important?"

"Not necessarily, but it would help us understand who you are better."

"Oh. My father was in trade," Amanda finally spoke. "He made out very well during the war running supplies."

Chapter 4

"Well, are ya goin' in or not?" Cookie growled at Teddy. "Maybe you plan on starin' at the door until the girl comes out."

Teddy twisted his hat in his hand, the familiar hard billed cap offering no comfort. "What if she turns me away?"

"You didn't haul your mattress to the bench of this old wagon and endure the trip to town to stand on the stoop worrin' boy, just go in and talk at her."

Teddy shuffled his feet but didn't move. How could he face the pretty Amanda? He was sure she hated him after what he had done. If only he had a bit more time with her that first day, things might be different.

"Scary is she?" Cookie laughed, climbing down from the buckboard. "Well, let me see for myself." The old man pushed open the door, swaggering into the boarding house.

Teddy felt the air leave his lungs. What would Cookie do? The old man was known for his quick tongue and attitude. Hurrying forward, Teddy followed the man into the dining area that faced the street.

"Well howdy, Miss Peri," Cookie all but shouted across the room. "Is this the new filly in town?" The old man stomped his way to a table where Jacks Verone and Mercy Perkins were having tea as they were introduced to Amanda. "She sure is a pretty little thing," Cookie continued.

Amanda looked up at the dusty old man with the scraggly beard and food-stained shirt. He was missing several teeth from his broad smile, and his eyes seemed foggy and dim.

"Hello Cookie," Peri stood from where she had been bending over the table. "This is Miss Antonia, newly arrived from Virginia."

Teddy watched in horror as Cookie took a turn around the young woman. "She's a might skinny, ain't she?" the old man asked. "Nice skin, though."

Teddy hurried toward the table, his ears going bright red at the horrified look on Amanda's face.

"I'll tell ya what," Cookie said, reaching out and plucking at the lace cuff on Amanda's pale pink dress. "How's about I take her off your hands. I never had a wife before and a nice young thing like this would keep me warm at night."

Teddy saw all the blood drain from Amanda's face, and he hurried to her side, afraid she might faint.

"Cookie, keep a civil tongue in your mouth around a lady." Teddy's tone was harsh, surprising even himself. "Miss Amanda, you look like you could use a bit of fresh air," he continued, laying her hand on his arm. "Would you step outside?"

Amanda looked between Teddy and the old reprobate who was ogling her with his rheumy eyes. "Thank you." She squeaked, grasping Teddy's proffered arm. "I do feel a bit light-headed."

"Cookie, why don't you have a seat," Jacks gave the old cattle cook a hard look, flicking his eyes to an empty chair as Mercy began humming *Bringing in the Sheaves* beside him. "I think you've made enough noise for the day."

Cookie's sharp cackle filled the room as he slapped his knee. "I reckon you're right," he laughed. "I reckon you're right."

***

Teddy steered Amanda out the front door past the stony glares of several men who were having their dinner. "Would you like to have a seat?" he asked gently, nodding toward a bench on the front porch.

Amanda covered her heart with a lace gloved hand, her eyes fluttering. "No, thank you." She managed, still trying to recover from her horror at the old man's proposition. The scruffy old coot was old enough to be her grandfather, or maybe even her great-grandfather. "Can we walk?"

"Yes, ma'am." Teddy's voice was gentle. "Now, don't you get a fright if some fella's come whoopin' through town," he added. "I'm here, and I'll look out for you."

Amanda's already wide blue eyes grew wider. "What kind of town is this?" she quavered. "Isn't anyone in this town civilized?"

Teddy shoved his hat back onto his head, giving himself a moment to think. "I guess that depends on your definition of civilized." He helped Amanda down the steps of the boardwalk as they crossed an alley. "Folks around here are still adjusting to Needful being a town."

The young man scratched his head, trying to find the right words. "Why not so long ago it was nothing but a trading post full of wild cowboys, Indians, and a few vaqueros from down south."

Amanda gasped, and Teddy steadied her on his arm. "We got law now, don't you worry. Sheriff Spencer Gaines is on the job."

"But everything is so wild, and we're so far from, from everywhere." Amanda felt utterly disoriented, and the old man had given her such a fright. Would she end up with someone like that? Was that the lot of a mail-order bride? Peri had said she found love in Needful.

"But we got each other," Teddy grinned, feeling her flinch under his hand. "I mean the town," he added with a blush. "Folks here in Needful tend to pull together when times are rough. Like when them bandits kidnapped Rosa and Ruth early this summer."

Amanda felt herself sway, and Mr. Lewis wrapped an arm around her protectively. "Bandits?"

Teddy eased the young woman through the door of the general store, settling her in a seat by the door. "Easy there now," he crooned. "They're all in jail now, nothing to worry about."

Amanda blinked at the young man. Perhaps he had carried her home with him, but he was a welcome alternative to the old man back at the boarding house.

"Teddy, what's wrong?" a tiny dark-haired woman hurried toward him.

"Mrs. Scripts, this is Miss Antonia, I'm afraid Needful is a bit of a shock to her. Would you fetch her a cup of water?" Teddy patted Amanda's hand tenderly as she closed her eyes, leaning against the back of the chair.

"I'm so sorry," Amanda whispered. "I don't know what's wrong with me. Everything is so overwhelming."

Teddy squeezed her hand. "You'll adjust," he assured. "Just take it slow and let folks help. We might be a bit needful here in this cow town, but that don't mean we aren't friendly and helpful."

Amanda opened her eyes, meeting Teddy's, a smile tugging at her lips at his quip. The young man was familiar, and his hand in hers seemed to fill her with strength.

"Here, drink this." The tiny woman returned, a tin cup in her hand.

Taking the cup from Mrs. Scripts, Teddy lifted it to Amanda's lips. "Go easy," he whispered, helping her drink.

Amanda lifted her hand, taking the cup and sipping. The cold water seemed to go straight to her head and she sighed, feeling better.

"Thank you," her eyes met Teddy's and his grin zipped to her heart. Perhaps the man wasn't as bad as she had thought. A shiver ran down her spine as she thought back to the old man and his rude comments at the boarding house.

"Feeling better?" Teddy watched as the young woman sat up a little straighter.

"Yes, I'm afraid I was unprepared for this town."

"Well, don't you let it worry your pretty little head," Teddy said. "I'll look out for ya. Now, how about a treat? Mrs. Scripts and her husband keep a right nice selection of hard candies."

Amanda felt the smile tugging at her lips. "That would be lovely," she agreed, looking around at the general store. The place was nothing like the fine shops she was used to back home, and suddenly she longed for home, where only a few months ago her father would have been buying her a lovely iced-cream.

"You sit right here," Teddy pushed to his feet and headed for the counter.

Amanda lifted the cup to her lips again, drinking the last of the water and feeling somewhat refreshed as she looked around her. Finding her feet, she ambled between tables full of leather and cloth goods, barrels of meal, flour, sugar, and beans. The store seemed to have all the basics one might need, but little else.

"You're feeling better," the tiny woman popped up from behind the counter where she had been filling a small brown bag with treats. "Do you need anything?"

Amanda shook her head, looking at Teddy. He had been kind to her, helpful, and protective when she felt wobbly. Perhaps he wasn't the scoundrel she had believed.

"I need a new hat," the young man admitted with a sheepish grin. "I'm afraid I lost mine the other day."

A quick laugh leapt to Amanda's lips, surprising her, and she covered her mouth with her hand. She had seen how Mr. Lewis had lost his hat, and her eyes dropped to the seat of his pants for a split second, making her face flame.

"I thought you just got a new hat last month." Mrs. Script queried.

"I lost it," Teddy bit out the words as his face heated. He didn't want to think about the embarrassing acts of only two days ago.

"If you'd like to go back to the boarding house, I can come back here later," Teddy offered, taking the paper bag from Mrs. Script and handing her some money.

"No, you go ahead." Amanda turned to look at the shelves again. "I'll look around here a bit." The young woman lifted her chin. "I need to start adjusting to my new home."

Teddy's smile was bright as he offered the bag of sweets to the young woman, watching as she picked out a lemon drop. Perhaps Miss Amanda was a delicate flower, but she had pluck, and he suspected that if she were planted in the right ground and tended with loving care, she would blossom into something more than the pretty bud before him.

"Hats," Mrs. Script grinned, hurrying around the counter. "Let's take a look."

For the next ten minutes, Teddy was busy trying on new hats. He had tried several on, each time looking to see if Amanda had anything to say, but she had simply looked at him, with little expression at all.

"This is the last one that might fit you," Mrs. Scripts spoke, handing down a light brown wide-brimmed hat. "It's been on the shelf a while, and I can give you a discount."

Teddy took the hat, examining the raised brim and wide leather band around the edge. "It's rather heavy."

"Yes, it is." Mrs. Scripts agreed, her tone flat.

Teddy slipped the hat on his head, turning this way and that to see that it fit snuggly enough not to blow off in the wind.

"That looks very nice on you," Amanda said, offering Teddy a smile that stabbed him in the heart.

"You like it?"

"It suits you."

"Here, look." Mrs. Scripts hurried back around the counter, pulling out a small handheld mirror.

Teddy examined his reflection in the mirror. He wasn't much to look at, in fact, plain would suit him: brown hair, brown eyes, slim, not too tall, or short, or skinny or fat just average.

"It looks nice," Amanda offered again.

"I'll take it," Teddy's eyes met Miss Antonia's, and a smile tugged at his lips. "I believe the lady has good taste." Perhaps a heavy hat was not the best for working in the hot Texas sun, but it would be worth it to see that smile again.

Teddy paid for the hat then offered Amanda his arm as he stuffed his ragged war cap in his back pocket with a groan. "Would you like to see the rest of the town?" he asked, offering her another sweet.

Amanda stepped out onto the covered boardwalk and squinted into the afternoon sun. "Is there much to see?"

"Not much," Teddy admitted. "Down that way is the church and across the street is the only saloon in town. That's where those rowdy cowboys are headed most of the time."

"Does it happen often? The shooting, I mean." Amanda shivered, remembering the fright she had received on arriving in Needful.

"Not so much as before," Teddy pointed down the street in the opposite direction. "The sheriff lives right there, and Spencer keeps a tight rein on things. Dan's had to bail several hands out of the hoosgow. Mayor Dan finally laid down the law and told the fellas that if they got arrested for disorderly conduct, they would not have a job."

"Did it work?"

"For the most part, yes," Teddy smiled. "You'll always have those saddle tramps that waste every dime in a saloon, though."

"And you?" Amanda met Teddy's dark eyes boldly.

"No ma'am. I've been with Cap'n, I mean Mayor Dan, for a long while. I'd not like to disappoint him."

Taking the man's proffered arm, Amanda

glanced over at him as he studied the street. His face, in profile, was serious, and a dark light flickered in his eyes.

"Thank you for the walk," Amanda offered as they arrived at the front of the boarding house. "Perhaps," she dropped her eyes, studying the dusty boards beneath her soft white boots. "Perhaps we can do this again."

Teddy bent over the young woman's hand. "I'd like that very much." He looked up, capturing her eyes. "I hope this means you can forgive me for being an idiot before."

Amanda grinned at the bright blush on the young man's face. "I'll think about it. Just keep that old man away from me."

Teddy chuckled. He had already noticed that the buckboard was gone and deducted that Cookie had headed for the store for supplies.

"That I can do."

***

"What just happened?" Olive asked, looking between Peri and Jacks, as Mercy continued to hum. "I thought that girl didn't want anything to do with Teddy Lewis."

"Looks like the boy beats the alternative," Jacks

laughed. "Cookie put a scare in that girl worse than Teddy ever could."

Mercy, smacked Jacks on the wrist gently, giving him that crooked grin.

"Mama, are you tired? Would you like to go home? Jacks can take you home, and Bear can collect me here when he's done if you're ready to go."

Mercy Perkins nodded slowly, her bright eyes twinkling. "Home," she said. "T'ank for da tea," she added as she reached for Olive's hand.

"You know you're welcome any time, Mercy." Olive rose still wondering about Cookie's quick departure through the back door, and Amanda's seeming, change of heart.

"Miss Mercy," Jacks pulled Mrs. Perkin's chair back, letting her grasp his arm as she rose. "Miss Peri, I'll see you later. Olive," he finished placing his hat on his head and tugging at it.

"It's a good thing Jacks has the time to ferry mother about," Peri said. "I'm glad she isn't stuck at home all the time. I mean, I know she has Prim and the house is always busy, but it's important to have people around that are closer to your age."

"I suppose that's true," Olive agreed. "You're mother is looking well. How is Prim?"

She seems fine. "I think expecting agrees with her."

"Your sister was our first bride here in Needful. Things sure have come a long way since then."

"I thought Daliah was the first bride."

"No, she and Spencer were the first wed once we arrived. Primrose came to us as a bride."

Peri giggled, thinking back to when her sister had agreed to come to Needful after reading an ad in a newspaper back home in Tennessee.

"Our lives certainly have changed since that day we cleaned out the cabin and moved in with Aunt Betsy," Peri agreed. "I wonder what Pa would say about us now." As much as Peri didn't approve of the life her father had led, she still missed the old moonshiner. His death had been what necessitated Prim's answering the advertisement.

Olive and Peri chatted a while longer, surprised when Amanda returned with a smile on her lips.

"Everything all right?" Olive asked the young woman.

"I'm feeling much better now," Amanda said, taking the seat Peri offered. "Mr. Lewis took me to the general store, and the fresh air seems to have done wonders for me."

"How 'bout a fresh pot of tea?" Olive leaned over the table with a grin.

"In this heat, I wish it were shaved ice." Amanda stripped off her gloves, folding them in her lap. "Tea will be fine," she finally added. "You've been most hospitable."

Olive grinned. "You do have nice manners," the older woman said. "We'll find you a nice man with a good place where you'll be looked after."

Amanda looked between Peri and Olive questioning who they might find in Needful who met those requirements, even as a set of serious dark eyes flashed before her. Perhaps Teddy Lewis had been rash in his behavior earlier, but he had been a complete gentleman today.

The cowboy's quick rescue of her from the derelict old man, foremost in his chivalrous behavior, had gained him points in her eyes.

"Who are all these men?" she asked delicately, peering at the men eating their lunches, who were staring at her with bold gazes.

"Just men," Olive said. "We have ranchers, cowboys, miners, and traders galore about these parts. Most are curious about any young woman who arrives. Many have even placed a request for a good woman of their own."

Amanda squirmed under the scrutiny of the men in the dining room. It was disconcerting being stared at in such a way.

"We've all been through it," Peri assured. "These men are hard-working and lonely. That's why Olive named the town Needful."

"I didn't mean anyone to hear that, but Orville, Periwinkle, and you know it."

Peri laughed, a soft, cheery titter in the staid room. "So I hear, but that don't mean it didn't stick."

"How did you name the town?" Amanda sat up, peering at Olive inquisitively. "Do tell."

"Well, it was our first big town meeting when Mayor Dan was elected. You could look around the town and see that ninety percent of the population was all men. Diggers, ropers, riders, and the such. The town had land, resources, a few fair buildings, but what it didn't have was good, respectable women. It was in need, in need of women and wives for these hard-working men."

"Daliah says that Olive here was talking to Orville as the meeting hushed and everyone heard her say that the town was Needful of good women."

"That's pretty much it," Olive agreed with a

shake of her head. "Dan heard me say it and put the name to a vote right then and there. It seems folks were willing to go with it."

Amanda laughed, thinking over what Mr. Lewis had told her about the town. Perhaps it was only going through the typical growing pains of any place on the edge of the frontier. Perhaps time would tell if Needful got all it had need of.

Chapter 5

"Cookie, what on earth were you thinking?" Teddy gave the old man a harsh look as he helped load the wagon. "You nearly scared Miss Amanda half to death."

The old man chuckled. "She ain't so scared of you now, though, is she?" Cookie chuckled.

"Why you rotten old coot," Teddy gaped. "You did that on purpose."

"You're kinda slow, ain't ya, son? What would an old man like me need with a pretty young wife? I ain't never needed a wife before, and I sure don't need one now. You, on the other hand, you're half smitten with that girl already. Now she knows there's worse things could happen than bein' hitched to a half-wit like yourself, she might come around."

Teddy pulled himself onto the padded seat of the wagon, still bewildered by the old man. It was true if Cookie hadn't gone into the Hampton House nattering on about taking a bride, Miss

Amanda Antonia would never have joined him outside.

"I ain't as dumb as you look, son," Cookie chuckled, slapping the reins to the horses and heading out of town. "You mark my words, you come calling again in a few days, and little Miss Amanda will look at you all different like."

Teddy pressed his hands onto the bench, flinching as the wagon rolled over a deep rut. He sure liked the idea of the sweet little miss being his wife. He would protect her, watch out for her, and let her know she was safe. A soft smile played about his lips as he imagined Amanda living in his home, cooking his meals, and sitting with him in the evening around a quiet fire.

"You think she'd be receptive-like to my callin'?" Teddy asked.

"She's young, alone, and you ain't half bad on the eyes, even if you are neigh unto hollow between the ears," Cookie said. "I reckon she's met you twice now, which is more than any of the others in town can say. You go on in and call on her in a day or two and see how it goes."

Teddy leaned back, crossing his arms over his chest with a grin, only to half stand as they rolled through another dip in the road.

Maybe, just maybe, he had a chance yet with

Miss Amanda Antonia. Teddy was tired of being alone, especially now that Mayor Dan had married Rosa. The men at the ranch spent more time in the bunkhouse, or on their small places, rather than lounging about the big ranch house.

Soon Dan would have children of his own, and Teddy thought that was a grand idea. What if he married Amanda and their children could play with Dan and Rosa's children. A soft blush warmed his face and Teddy settled back on the padded seat.

"Don't go gettin' the cart before the horse now boy," Cookie grinned. "It's one thing to convince a woman to marry you, it's another to keep her happy."

Teddy shot a scathing look at the old man. "How would you know?" he asked. "You ain't never been hitched."

"I got my reasons," Cookie growled. "They just ain't none of your business."

***

It took two more days before Teddy was fit to sit his pretty pony, and he headed into town. He'd dusted his best shirt, put on clean trousers, and placed his new hat carefully over his neatly combed hair.

"How do I look?" the young man asked Rosa as he shuffled to the house to retrieve the flowers his boss's wife had prepared.

"You look, muy handsome," Rosa smiled. "I wish you luck."

Teddy blushed, tugging at his string tie self consciously. "You think she'll approve?"

"This, I do not know," Rosa sighed. "I do not know this girl. I know that you are a good man and a good friend to Daniel." Rosa's lilting voice, accented with the tongue of her motherland, was almost musical. "If she is the right woman for you, all will be well."

Teddy nodded, mumbling a thank you to the dark-haired woman, then strode to his horse and stepped into the saddle, flowers clutched firmly in his hand.

"Don't do nothin' I wouldn't, Teddy," Dozer, a big man with a slow drawl, shouted as he started from the ranch yard.

"You talk real sweet now and maybe that girl will ignore them jug handle ears of yours," another cowboy offered.

"Just don't try to sing her a song," a third rider called as Teddy kicked his horse into a trot. "You'll be sure to scare her back home with your caterwauling."

Teddy felt the heat rise up his neck at the joshing of his friends and fellow riders. He knew he wouldn't get away with courting, completely unscathed by their acid wit. He just hoped that none of what they said was true. He barely knew how to talk to the young woman as it was, let alone win her hand.

Easing his pony to a walk, Teddy straightened his tie and ambled toward town. "Maybe I should make up a poem," he spoke to his black and white pinto. "Women like poems, don't they?"

Pepper snorted as if dismissing the thought and Teddy blushed again as the only poem he could recall was not fit for a delicate young lady like Amanda's ears.

"I'll take her to dinner," The young man grinned then sagged as he realized the only place to eat in town was where she lived. "That won't work." Beneath him, the painted pony shook its head with a derogatory snort. "Well, what does a body do for courtin' a woman in a town like Needful then?"

Teddy looked down at his horse's black and white mane but this time, the animal remained silent.

***

AMANDA

"Amanda, you have a caller." Ellen Hampton tapped on Amanda's door. "You don't have to see him if you don't want to."

Amanda opened the door of her spartan room and peered at the other woman. Ellen had been very kind to her since her arrival, not that the others hadn't been kind. Ellen just seemed friendlier.

"You do have the prettiest things," Ellen said, looking down at the young woman's powder blue dress.

"Thank you," Amanda smiled. "Who, who did you say is calling?"

Ellen grinned, seeing the fear in the girl's eyes. "It's just Teddy. Teddy Lewis."

"Oh, thank goodness," Amanda gasped, then covered her mouth. "I'm sorry, I shouldn't have said that."

"You're just glad it isn't Cookie," Ellen laughed. "I can't say as I blame you."

Amanda smiled, walking to the small cupboard to retrieve her gloves. "I think I'd like to see Teddy," she said. "Could you let him know I'll be right down?"

"I will," Ellen grinned. "I can arrange for you

two to sit in the parlor of Mother Hampton's quarters if you'd like."

Amanda looked up, feeling the nerves building in her stomach. "I'll let you know."

Minutes later, Amanda walked down the steps of the Hampton House, smiling when she saw Teddy standing at the bottom, a bouquet of wildflowers in his hands.

"Miss Antonia," the young man drawled, pulling his new hat from his head.

Amanda smiled, wondering for a moment just how old Teddy Lewis was. His face was youthful, but his eyes seemed so old, and the dark light behind them seemed to tug at her heart.

"Good afternoon," Amanda greeted, accepting the flowers from Teddy's rough hands.

"I hope you don't mind. I came callin'," Teddy shuffled his freshly polished boots. "I thought perhaps we could go for a walk."

"That would be lovely," Amanda agreed, surprising herself. She hadn't stepped outside the Hampton house since she had seen him last.

"Let me take those," Ellen hurried to Amanda taking the bundle of wildflowers. "I'll put these in a vase for your room."

Teddy offered Amanda his arm, leading her toward the front door.

"Theodore Lewis, what are you doing here?" Olive bustled into the dining room, looking between Teddy and Amanda. "Don't you think you've done enough harm?"

"It's all right, Mrs. Hampton," Amanda smiled. "Mr. Lewis offered to take me for a walk."

Olive flicked her dark eyes to the young man. "Well, no shenanigans," she grumbled, wagging a finger in Teddy's direction.

"Yes, Ma'am," Teddy agreed, picking up the pace before Olive could interfere. "I'll be the perfect gentleman. I just thought Miss Amanda, I mean Miss Antonia might like to see the rest of the town."

Olive placed her hands on her hips and scowled, but Amanda seemed content to go with the young man. "Be back for supper," she ordered. "I don't suppose anything major can happen, walking through Needful."

Amanda stepped out into the bright sun of the day and sighed as the fresh hot air wafted around her, like satin caressing her skin.

"It's very warm," she commented.

"It's finally starting to cool off a bit," Teddy corrected. "Not that it ain't warm."

"It gets very warm in Virginia as well," Amanda's words were polite. "What do people do around here for fun?"

Teddy paused, looking up and down the dusty street. A couple of cowboys ambled out of town, their horses moving at a sedate pace, an old miner trudged toward the general store, a broken pick-axe in his hand, and a skinny dog slunk down a dark alley.

"I don't rightly know," Teddy admitted. "There's them that goes to the saloon, and on Sunday the town all turns out to church. We've even had a few picnics and socials after weddings." Teddy ducked his head, feeling his ears flush as he thought of possibly marrying the pretty woman on his arm.

"What about dances or tea parties?" Amanda asked as Teddy stepped out once more. "Wouldn't the men like a good dance?"

"I reckon they would, but who would they dance with? I reckon men outnumber women here three to one. Why you ladies would be danced plumb off your feet."

"I see your point." Amanda worried the lace kerchief in her hand as they continued down the

AMANDA

boardwalk. "It's a shame, though. I always enjoyed the parties my family had. They were lively, with good music, dancing, and fancy food."

Teddy stopped, this time turning to look into Amanda's face. "Why'd you come to Needful if you had all that back home?"

Amanda dropped her eyes again. "I don't like to speak ill of people," she hedged.

"You can tell me," Teddy urged, placing his finger under her chin and lifting her eyes to his. "I'm your friend."

Amanda tried to smile as all the events of the past few months came rushing back.

"My father died about eight months ago," she said, tears pooling behind her eyes. "He was a hard man, but honest and fair in his dealings. He had a good business in shipping before the unpleasantness between the states, but during that time, his earnings shot straight up." Amanda didn't like talking about the vulgarities of money, but she needed Teddy to understand why she had come to Needful.

"I'm sorry for your loss," Teddy said, his voice full of compassion. "Both my folks was lost in the war."

Amanda reached out, squeezing Teddy's hand in

sympathy. "Mother, well, Mother didn't seem to know what to do when father passed. She became quite odd, and soon an old friend of my father was sitting at supper with us nearly every night. They, they married two months ago." Amanda's face burned with horror at the social faux pas. "It was rather scandalous."

"Why?" Teddy asked. "Don't your mother deserve some happiness? I'm afraid too many unwed and widowed women are still without a man about the house in some states. It's a bitter pill to swallow."

"I'm sorry," again, Amanda dropped her eyes. "I shouldn't have said anything."

Teddy studied the young woman a moment longer taking in the stiff spine, and hunched shoulders. "Was that the whole of it?" he asked, his voice gentle.

Amanda looked up her blue eyes wide as she stared at Teddy. "I saw him in town with another woman."

Teddy felt the blood roar to his head at Amanda's words and he pulled her to his side protectively. "That ain't right," he drawled. "Not right at all. Why if I'd been there," he shook his fist, indicating what he would have done. "Did you tell your mother?"

Amanda shook her head. "I tried to say something, but Mother was smitten and then there were the boys to worry about. Mother had married the man and legally, he had a claim to all we owned. I decided it would be better to leave."

Teddy held one of Amanda's gloved hands in his, wrapping the other arm around her back. "You're safe with me," he whispered. "Don't you never fear."

Amanda didn't know why, but Teddy's words seemed to sink into her soul, giving her confidence she had never known. She had grown up with society's staid boundaries, but now that they had all been stripped away, she felt utterly adrift in this new world.

"Thank you," she looked up, meeting his gaze as a strange comfort seemed to envelop her. Despite the young man's rash behavior upon her arrival, he was proving that he was indeed a friend and protector.

"I'm glad you called, Mr. Lewis," she smiled. "I believe that we are coming to an understanding of one another."

Teddy beamed, hoping that those words would lead them down the center aisle of the little white church on the edge of town before anyone else could interfere.

Teddy walked Amanda to the end of town, then crossed the street and began the walk back. The young woman hung on his arm, and he felt like the luckiest man in town with such a lovely thing to escort.

Teddy had no allusions about his good looks, special talents, or wealth. He was a simple cowhand who knew how to work hard. He had learned the trade after arriving here with Cap'n Dan. Over the past few years, he had built a cabin, set aside a few dollars for emergencies, and settled into a simple life among friends.

"Miss Antonia," he said as they approached the Hampton House, stopping to gaze across the street at the two-story building made of hand-hewn logs. "I know I ain't much, but I'm a hard worker. I've been on my own a long while now, and I'm tired of it. I want a home, a family, a woman to call my own. Someone who can be a friend and comfort. I know I'm not rich or handsome, but I am loyal. You can ask anyone, and they'll tell you I stand by those I care for. I know it's early yet, but I'd like you to consider my suit for your hand. I don't see no reason to beat about the bush. I asked Olive to get me a bride, and from what you say, you need someone who will stand by you. You don't need to decide on nothin' now, but I hope that perhaps you'll consider me as a possible match."

Amanda felt her cheeks heat again, but she didn't cringe away from the man. There was a deep honesty in his words, and if truth be told, she found his appearance rather appealing.

"I'll consider it," Amanda agreed. "I can't live at the Hampton House forever."

Teddy nodded, feeling her words in his chest. He understood that if Amanda accepted him, it wouldn't be out of love, but necessity. She needed a protector, a home, security, all things he could offer. Perhaps she was used to fine things and fancy parties, but he was sure if he worked hard enough, he could make the young woman happy in his simple home.

"I think Olive is looking for us," Amanda smiled, nodding toward the window at the front of the boarding house. "She'll expect us to supper."

"We'd best not keep her waiting then," Teddy grinned, taking her arm and stepping into the street. "We wouldn't want to upset Mrs. Hampton. Not with that brood of men she's got about."

Amanda's quick laugh lifted Teddy's heart, and he sent a prayer to heaven that she could be his. He felt that he understood her need for a new home and a new start and was willing to give her everything he had, including his heart.

"Did you have a nice walk?" Olive asked, studying the pair as they stepped through the door. "It seems a bit warm to be out traipsing about the streets."

"It was delightful," Amanda replied. "Thank you."

Teddy grinned. The girl certainly had nice manners. If they were to wed, would she teach his children such things?

"Why don't you two sit down," Olive asked, indicating a group of tables that had been put together for her family. "We might as well enjoy the food while it's hot."

"Yes, ma'am," Teddy agreed, hurrying toward Orville and his sons who sat with their families. Other men had gathered at various tables, enjoying the food as well.

Teddy pulled a chair out for Amanda, helping her take a seat as he hung his hat on a peg near the door. "It's a rare treat to sit with the family," Teddy whispered in her ear. "The food is good too. Not so spicy as Rosa's but good."

"I thought Cookie made the food at the ranch," Amanda scowled.

"Rosa used to work here at the Hampton House before she married Mayor Dan," Teddy grinned. "It's quite the tale, and one day, maybe she'll share it with you."

"Shall we pray?" Orville asked, reaching for the hands on either side of him as the family linked palms in preparation for the prayer.

Amanda placed her delicate hand in Teddy's rough one, and he felt a swoosh of energy run through him as he bowed his head in prayer.

***

"Ellen, would you mind helping me with my dress?" Amanda asked as the dinner dishes were cleared away.

Teddy had left shortly after dessert had been served, and Amanda couldn't' stop thinking about him or the conversation they had shared. Theodore Lewis, though not wealthy, seemed a good man.

"I'd be glad to help," Ellen smiled, leaning over to whisper in her husband's ear and giving a hard look to her two children. "Joe can see that the children finish their schoolwork and their chores."

Joseph Hampton grinned, offering his wife a wink. "I'll see to it, my dear," he said, leaning in and placing a kiss on her cheek. "I'll see you later."

Ellen blushed, but her face was passive as she watched her small family walk away. "Come on, then."

Amanda was thankful for the help as Ellen unbuttoned each tiny pearl down her spine. "I had to button all but the top few and shimmy into it this morning," she sighed as the dress came off. "I'm sorry to be such trouble."

"You're no trouble," Ellen grinned. "You had a need, and I was able to help."

Amanda turned, meeting Ellen's eyes. "Ellen, what do you think of Mr. Lewis?"

"He's a fine man," Ellen said without hesitation. "I know Mayor Dan trusts him, and he's a hard worker."

"Do you think he would make a good husband?" Amanda's face flamed, and she turned back to the bureau, pulling out her nightdress.

"Yes, I do." Ellen's straight forward answer caught Amanda by surprise. "But Olive and Peri think I need a man with a comfortable home and means to provide for me."

"Is that what you think?"

"I don't know," Amanda slipped the nightdress over her head and then reached behind her to undo her corset. "I think I like him, though."

Ellen grinned. "I can't say I felt the same the first

time I met Joe," she laughed.

"Really?" Amanda's eyes grew wide,

"No. Here stand up and let me help you with that." The other woman indicated the undergarment. "The first time I met Joe, there was just something about him that rubbed me the wrong way."

"What?"

"I don't know. The man bothered me. He was persistent, though, and soon I came to love the man I learned to know."

Amanda grinned, wondering if she could learn to love Theodore Lewis. "He is a good man, isn't he?"

"Yes," Ellen answered without hesitation. Joe was a wonderful husband and father.

"Ellen?" Amanda stepped out of the corset, letting her soft linen nightgown slip over her slight form. "If I were to marry Mr. Lewis, do you think I could come to love him?"

"I don't see why not," Ellen grinned. "It seems to me that love is not only a feeling but a decision. Each day we wake up, we have to decide to love that person we chose, or who chose us. Not every day is sunshine and roses, but if you choose to love each day, you'll muddle through."

"Is that how it is for you?" Amanda looked at her new friend with concern.

"Some days." Ellen met Amanda's eyes. "Some days, you don't feel like loving, or even very lovable, but that doesn't change the fact that you made a commitment and need to make it last. Today, Joe knew I wanted to help you, so he took the children. Another day he might want to go fishing with his brothers, and I'll see to things at home. There's a give and take to the rhythm of life."

"But, you're happy?"

"Oh, yes, I'm happy. I have moments when I'm not happy. I left my home and family to come here with Joe, but this is my place, and I know he loves me. Joe looks out for me, provides, and helps. I do the same for him. Sometimes he has to help me more and sometimes I have to help him. That builds strength and devotion."

"It doesn't sound very romantic."

"Sometimes it isn't," Ellen admitted. "Other times," she blushed brightly and grinned. "Other times it's romantic in a way that sweeps you off of your feet. Usually when you least expect it."

Amanda grinned, trying to imagine what it

would be like to have a man romance her. "Mr. Lewis did bring pretty flowers," she said, walking to the old crock that held the colorful offering on her nightstand. "That was rather thoughtful."

"I think, given half the chance, Teddy would be just that. Thoughtful." Ellen squeezed Amanda's arm. "Take your time and pray about it all," she said. "God will direct you in the path that you should go."

"Thank you," Amanda grabbed Ellen, hugging the other woman on impulse. "I can't tell you how helpful you've been. I'll take my time and think on all of this until the next time Mr. Lewis calls."

Ellen hugged the girl back. She seemed so small, frail, and unprepared for a place like Needful, but she had come here with her own needs, and Ellen wouldn't pry.

"We'll keep you in our prayers as well," Ellen smiled. "You're here now, and we'll believe this is just where God wants you."

Amanda blinked at Ellen for several seconds. She hadn't thought about God's will in this matter. When she had answered the ad and booked her passage, she had only one thought in mind, escape.

"I hope you're right," she spoke, her words soft as Ellen slipped through the door.

Amanda sat on the edge of the bed, looking at the flowers on the stand. They were simple, unlike the flowers she had seen almost daily in her mother's home, but they seemed more precious than all the hothouse roses money could buy.

Chapter 6

Teddy pulled the old harmonica from his breast pocket and blew through it, settling back in the saddle as Pepper made his way home. As his lips once more became familiar with the instrument, a soft tune lilted into the night.

It had been a long time since Teddy had played the mouth organ. He had played often on those long nights when he and Dan's crew had first arrived on this patch of soil that would eventually become Needful.

Long days and lonely nights had pulled sad songs and old ballads from Teddy's war-weary soul, and he had often taken requests from his friends and fellow soldiers, but tonight a sweet tune of promise issued from the battered, tin and reed, noisemaker; A song of love and romance.

Teddy's heart lifted on the tune, willing it to carry the miles back to town and flutter into Amanda's heart. Today, he had spoken his mind, and the young woman hadn't run or even laughed at him. He felt that perhaps if she would agree to marry him, they could be friends, companions, and eventually lovers.

It had been many years since Teddy had known the love of a real family, and though Dan and his crew were as close to family as Teddy had, he knew that in his heart, he had a great deal of love to share with that perfect someone.

A smile broke his concentration, and Teddy changed the tune to a familiar dance song from his younger days. He remembered his mother kicking up her heels on the dance floor with his father, their bright eyes and happy smiles filling his young heart with joy. Teddy had never doubted his parents' affection for him or each other, but they had succumbed to the ravages of war and the illness that followed famine before he could return home.

"I could have a love of my own," Teddy whispered into the night sky. "Someone to have and to hold." Amanda's bright eyes and pretty face drifted before him, and he pressed the harmonica back to lips that longed to kiss her.

He would return to Needful in a few days and see if Amanda had considered his proposal. Teddy knew that if Miss Antonia married him, he could protect, provide, and care for her.

His home wasn't much, but in time he could add on. He had a little saved, not being wasteful, or one who rollicked in the saloon. In time, if he worked hard and was careful, he could give Amanda the finer things in life that she was used to. Perhaps not to the extent she had known growing up, but wasn't security, affection, and love more important than things?

Again, a sweet love song trilled into the night as the lights of the ranch came into view.

Was this how love started? Teddy wondered, with a wish, a hope, and a prayer.

"Teddy, is that you?" Dan's voice echoed out across the yard as Pepper headed for the barn, the soft tones of the harmonica floating on the breeze.

"It's me Cap'."

Dan shook his head, stepping off the front porch and walking toward the pony that angled toward the barn. "I heard you comin'. It's been a while since we had a tune from you."

Teddy stepped down from his pony, slipping the harmonica back into his pocket. "I haven't felt much like playing lately."

"Seemed a happy tune, from what I could hear."

Teddy felt his face flush and was thankful for the

darkness to hide his red cheeks. "I'd about forgotten those tunes."

"I take it you had a nice day?"

Teddy twisted his head, looking over his shoulder as he loosened the straps on Pepper's saddle. "Can't say it was bad."

"You like this girl?"

Teddy stood, turning toward his boss as Pepper huffed in disgust at the delay. "I do," he admitted seriously, wondering if Dan had something to say on the issue. "Is that a problem?"

"No, no," Dan grinned. "Nothing wrong with it in my book. You just walk easy is all. I wouldn't want to see you get hurt."

Teddy lifted his chin. "I don't see how it's of any mind to you," he said. "I reckon I like the girl, and if she's of a mind, I'll ask her to marry me."

Dan's eyebrows rose. He had his fill of trouble fighting his emotions when it came to Rosa, who was he to question Teddy. "All right," he said, slapping the younger man on the shoulder. "I'll wish you the best and leave it at that."

Teddy's bright smile was visible even in the dim light from the stars. "Thanks, Cap'n."

"Would you stop calling me that?" Dan grumbled. "I'm not a captain anymore. I'm just Dan. Dan Gaines, reluctant mayor of Needful, Texas."

Teddy chuckled. "That's the truth. You never did want the position, but you're doin' a good job."

"Thanks, Teddy." Dan turned back to look at his house. He could see Rosa in the window of the top floor tucking Christina into bed and his heart swelled. He hadn't planned on marrying the beautiful young woman or building a big house, or most any of the things he had done since settling in the hill country of Texas.

"You'd best put Pepper, up," Dan laughed as the pony sidled toward the barn and a good feed. "I think he's done with this day, whether we are or not."

"Thanks, Dan." Teddy grinned, snatching the reins of his pony and stripping the saddle with one hand. "I'll do that. Good night."

Dan waved, turning and walking back to the quiet house as Teddy headed for the barn. Things were changing fast around Needful and he wasn't sure how best to protect those under his care. Teddy was so young, and yet he had seen so much in his few years. Dan prayed the boy wasn't in for a world of hurt with the fancy little girl who had already stolen his heart.

***

"Has Mr. Lewis called?" Amanda asked Olive a few days after Teddy's visit. "He said he would call again."

"Now don't you worry about Teddy, he's a young man and will be along in time. For now, why don't you sit with me, and we'll talk about someone who might suit you and your specific needs?"

Amanda flicked her eyes to the floor in shame. She had understood that she was to help around the Hampton House to pay for room and board, but so far, she had not been of any real use. Only yesterday, she had dropped a tray full of food when a dirty miner had tugged at her sleeve, offering her a toothless grin. The day before, she had boiled a pot of tea dry, and when asked to do the laundry, she had all but caught her skirt tail on fire.

"Of course," Amanda complied, slipping into a chair. "I'd rather not have anyone old."

Olive chuckled, after Cookie's appearance a few days earlier the young woman had become even jumpier than she already was. "There are only a few men I think might be suitable for you," Olive began. "They are a bit older than you, but that means they are more established."

Amanda's eyes grew wide, envisioning an old toothless soul with a scraggly beard. Teddy's handsome face popped into her mind, and she twisted her hands together in her lap. Perhaps Teddy wasn't every girl's dream, but at least he was young and seemed sincere in his desire to protect her. He lived on that big ranch and had steady work.

"Amanda, are you listening?" Olive, hunched low over the table, peered up into the young woman's face.

"Yes, Ma'am."

Olive droned on chatting about someone with a small music business, and Amanda's mind drifted again. It would indeed be better to marry Mr. Lewis than being auctioned off to some old man who thought of her as nothing more than a pretty bauble. At least Theodore Lewis seemed to hold some affection for her.

"Teddy Lewis is here." Arabela swept into the room, blue eyes twinkling in a classically beautiful face. "He's asking for you, Amanda."

Amanda sprang to her feet. "If you'll excuse me," she squeaked, hurrying past the black-haired woman. "I'll see him now."

A wide smile spread across Teddy's face as Amanda stepped into the dining area. She was as pretty as could be in a light green dress with a fancy waterfall cascade down the back.

"Hello," her greeting was shy.

"Miss Antonia," Teddy grinned. "I was wondering if you'd like to go for a buggy ride today and see the area."

Amanda nodded, her mind whirring. "That sounds fine," she smiled again. "I'll just fetch my parasol and be right down.

"I'll let Darwin know I need the buggy." Teddy hurried toward the back door as Amanda hurried up the stairs. "Darwin," he shouted across the dusty yard. "I need a buggy, wagon, cart, whatever you have."

A black-haired man with a neatly trimmed beard emerged from the still-new livery structure with a grin. "You goin' somewhere?" Darwin Rivers asked.

"I'm taking Miss Amanda for a ride," Teddy beamed.

"You don't say? She's a frilly little thing, isn't she?"

"I suppose," Teddy blustered. "Have you met her?"

"Yes, Ruth took to her straight away. It seems they had a lot to talk about with books and parties and the things ladies enjoy in certain circles."

Teddy looked over his shoulder to see if Amanda had followed him. "Do you have a buggy for me?"

"Sure, sure," Darwin grinned. "All I have is the cart, but it's nice and cozy." The other man's grin was devilish and Teddy felt his face flush.

"It will do, please bring it around to the front of the boarding house. I'll meet you there."

Darwin touched the brim of his hat with a chuckle, turning back to the barn.

"Mr. Lewis?" Amanda peered into the dining area as several men looked up and grinned.

"He ain't back," a man in a tattered coat offered. "I'd be happy to take you for a ride, though." The man's dark eyes glinted, and Amanda shrank back.

"I'd rent a buggy if you'd go out with me," another man offered. "We could get better acquainted."

Amanda felt her stomach turn and she clutched her parasol firmly, raising it like a weapon.

"There you are," Teddy slipped back into the house, his dark eyes darting toward the men ogling Amanda. "If you're ready, we can go." He offered his arm in a gentlemanly gesture, glaring at the others in the room.

Amanda grasped Teddy's arm, her fingers shaking as they swanned past the men, still gaping at her.

"Are you feelin' poorly?" Teddy asked, handing Amanda into the small two-wheeled cart. "We can stay here if you'd like."

"I'm fine," Amanda smiled down at him, reading the concern in his eyes. "I'm afraid the way those men look at me is rather disconcerting."

Teddy climbed into the narrow seat, his hip coming up against the young woman's skirt. "Well don't you worry about them, no man in these parts would harass a respectable woman. First, it just ain't done and second, they'd have to answer to Dan and Spencer Gaines."

Amanda smiled, feeling more at ease as Teddy chirruped to the horse, setting it off at a trot. "Oh," she gasped, grabbing the young man's strong arm, once more, to keep from tipping over the back of the seat.

"Sorry about that," Teddy blushed. "I didn't figure Darwin would give us a lively horse."

Amanda ducked her head but smiled. It was a beautiful day for a drive and a significant talk. She was happy to get away from the boarding house and out into the bright sunshine of the Texas hill country.

AMANDA

Teddy drove on, liking the way Miss Amanda's hand rested on his arm. She seemed thoughtful today, and he hoped she wasn't going to tell him that Olive had found a better match for her. In the short time, he had known the pretty Miss Antonia. Teddy had grown rather fond of her. Perhaps she was from a whole different world than he was, but she had come to Needful seeking a husband, and he knew, given half a chance, he could be the right man for her.

"Mr. Lewis," Amanda began, twirling her open parasol nervously. "Is what you said the other day on our walk true?"

"You mean about me liking you and hoping you'll agree to be my wife? Yes."

Amanda blushed but smiled. "Do you still mean it?"

"Of course." Teddy looked toward the young woman. "Are you fixin' to tell me you aren't interested?"

"No!" Amanda squeezed his arm, feeling him relax. "I've been considering it, that's all. Miss Olive is trying to find me someone more suitable, but I don't think anyone would be more suitable."

Teddy's eyes grew wide with disbelief, was Miss Amanda saying what he thought. "You mean you'll consider me?"

"Yes," Amanda smiled, the shade of her parasol, making her eyes glow a deeper blue. "I feel safe with you, and you aren't hard to look at. I'm afraid I'm not skilled in the art of homemaking, but I'm sure in time I'll learn."

Teddy lifted a fist in the air with hearty "whoop!" making the horse lunge into a canter and tossing Amanda almost into his lap. Ignoring the galloping horse, he pulled Amanda close and planted a firm kiss on her lips.

"Mr. Lewis!" Amanda gasped as he released her, her whole body filling with heat.

Teddy grasped the reins firmly in his hands, his face flaming red as he eased the horse back to a more sedate pace. "I'm sorry," he said. "I'm afraid I lost my head."

Amanda cast a sideways glance at the man next to her but grinned. "You're that pleased?" She had never been kissed and the man's enthusiasm seemed contagious.

"I am."

A sense of accomplishment and well being filled Amanda's heart. She would have her protector, one of her choosing.

***

"What do you mean you're getting married?" Olive gaped at Amanda, who stood quietly in the busy kitchen.

"I've decided that Mr. Lewis is the best choice for me," Amanda said. "We'll be married this afternoon. Mr. Lewis is speaking to the preacher now."

"But I thought you wanted someone more genteel." Olive stared at the girl. "Teddy's a good boy, but he's not able to give you pretty dresses, or a big house."

"I think Mr. Lewis and I will be well suited," Amanda blushed. "He's very attentive."

Olive squinted at the girl. "Did something happen on that buggy ride?"

"No, Ma'am." Amanda gaped. "I'm a proper lady." Again her cheeks heated. "He did kiss me, though."

"Good for you," Ellen walked into the room, an empty serving tray in her hands. "If you like Teddy, there's no reason you shouldn't marry him."

"Ellen," Olive huffed.

"Mother Hampton, you know she's a grown woman and able to make her own choices. Teddy's a good soul, and he likes her. Isn't that better than living with a man who sees you as a pretty object to be strutted about town?"

"Well, yes. I suppose so." Olive still wasn't convinced. "But why not wait and have a proper wedding. Sunday's only one day away."

"I don't think it would be right to take further advantage of your hospitality," Amanda's words were soft. "I'm of no use to you here and besides, all those men staring at me every day is quite disconcerting."

"You can't argue with that," Shililaih walked into the room, moving to the stove to retrieve a fresh pot of coffee. "The girl's completely out of place here. She might as well get hitched and start out in her new life."

"Shi!" Olive gasped.

"No, she's right." Amanda turned to look at the lovely Irish woman, with a name as sassy as her attitude. "I may not know how to do much for myself, but I will learn. I believe that Mr. Lewis will be patient with me and that he cares for me enough to see to my well being. It's time I grew up and learned to look after myself."

"When will the ceremony take place?" Olive asked in defeat.

"I'm sure Mr. Lewis will send word soon."

AMANDA

"I wish you had given us a bit of time," Olive grumbled. "A fine wedding would be quite the treat for the town, and it would show the other men that Peri and I do know what we're doing."

Ellen laughed, "Mother Hampton, why don't we let Amanda get ready. I'm sure she's brought a special dress for the occasion."

"Yes, I have," Amanda agreed, her blue eyes shining with excitement. "Could you help me dress, or are you too busy?" Amanda turned, looking at Ellen, hopefully.

"I'd be delighted." Ellen grasped Amanda's arm and turned toward the back stairs. "We'll get you ready for your big day."

"Ellen," Amanda asked a few minutes later as her friend and companion helped her out of her day dress. "Do you think I'm making a mistake?"

"That depends," Ellen smiled, running her hand over the delicate lace covering the pristine white satin of an exquisite gown, with a high collar and mutton sleeves.

"You think I'm rushing?"

"No, but if you don't think you can grow to care about Teddy, you shouldn't marry him."

Amanda chewed her bottom lip for a moment.

"I think I could care for him. At least he is closer in age to my own, and that gives us something in common."

"You don't have to rush." Ellen looked up knowingly.

"I think it's best if I just get on with it," Amanda said, showing some nerve. "There's no point putting off the inevitable, and I don't see any of the other men Olive has contracted with being more appealing than Mr. Lewis." The young woman shivered slightly with revulsion.

"Then I guess you've made the right choice."

Amanda smiled, feeling some of the tension melt away. "May I ask you another question?" the younger woman blushed, meeting Ellen's twinkling gaze.

"Don't tell me, your mama never explained about the wedding night."

Amanda's face went crimson as she shook her head, but she didn't turn away.

Ellen took Amanda's hand and set her down on the bed for the talk. Ellen took a moment ordering her thoughts for a conversation she believed she had years before she had to share. Her daughter had only turned eight a few weeks ago and had years before Ellen needed to explain love, but she still began.

Chapter 7

"You look like a dream!" Shililiah sighed as Amanda walked down the stairs, stepping lightly as Ellen held up the train of the beautiful dress.

"Oh my!" Olive gazed at the young woman. "I've never seen the like."

"Do you like it?" Amanda asked. "I bought it just before I left Virginia. It's from France."

"Mother?" Arabela gaped. "I think we are closed."

"Excuse me?" Olive turned to her tallest daughter-in-law.

"We're closed!" Arabela called, hurrying out to the dining hall. "Take your meals and leave, we have a wedding to attend."

Ellen and Shi laughed as the patrons gathered their things and left the room.

"I'm putting on my Sunday best. Please wait for us," Arabela chirped, her eyes bright as she gazed at Amanda stepping inside. "Ellen, send Jacob for the men. Today is going to be a day to remember."

Olive blinked for several seconds then jumped into gear. "Give us twenty minutes," she said, lifting her skirts and heading for the living quarters.

***

"You look lovely, dear." Orville Hampton patted Amanda's hand as they walked toward the church at the end of town. He'd donned his best suit after shutting down the sawmill for the rest of the day and urging his boys to put on their nice duds.

The whole family was turned out for the big event.

"Joseph, run on ahead and let Teddy know we're on our way." Olive urged her younger son.

"Thank you for this," Amanda looked around at the family, missing her younger brothers terribly. What would they say about her big adventure now? She had answered the ad in the paper with a letter to Olive, and left soon afterward, leaving her mother in tears. Now, she was getting married, and the Hamptons being at her side eased some of her heartache and homesickness.

***

Teddy turned as Joseph walked through the door. Pastor Tippert offered him a kind smile.

"Looks like the Hamptons will be joining us." The tall skinny preacher turned, grinning at Beth, his lovely young wife, as he brushed his unruly brown hair from his eyes.

"I'd say it's a proper wedding," Beth smiled back as Orville walked through the door with Amanda on his arm. The shimmering white confection of a dress she wore had layers of ruffles from the waist to the floor and gave the young woman an appearance of gliding down the aisle.

"Boy howdy, would you look at that," Teddy beamed. He stood in his best suit, the one he'd come calling in, but felt like a country mouse in comparison to the elegance that floated his way.

"Are we ready?" Brandon Tippert grinned as Teddy stared at the vision in white that stood before him.

"Yes," Amanda whispered, mesmerized by the glow in Teddy's eyes. "Mr. Lewis?"

"Yes? Yes," Teddy gave his head a shake and turned to the preacher as the Hamptons filled the front benches of the humble church.

Brandon cleared his throat, looking down at the little book in his hand, then paused, staring toward the back of the church where rugged men filtered through the door occupying the back rows.

"Welcome," Brandon grinned, as more and more of the town's folks walked through the doors to witness the wedding. "We are gathered here today, in the sight of God and many men," he grinned as the rough crowd shuffled to seats, "to join this man and this woman in holy matrimony."

Teddy squeezed Amanda's small hand in his, oblivious to what was going on at the back of the church. From the moment Orville had placed her hand in his, he had eyes for nothing other than Amanda Antonia.

Preacher Tippert nudged his arm, prompting him to say the words a groom was to say then turned to Amanda, who repeated her vows in a firm voice.

"We will now exchange the rings," Brandon said, looking at Teddy expectantly.

"I don't got a ring," Teddy blushed. "I'll get you one soon, though," he added, looking at Amanda, who pulled a glove from her hand, slipping a small signet from her finger.

"We can use this," she smiled. It didn't matter that Mr. Lewis had no ring for her. She was gaining a husband, companion, protector, and, hopefully, a friend.

Teddy's face flushed again, but he nodded, saying the words the preacher told him to as he placed the ring on Amanda's finger.

"By the powers vested in me by the great state of Texas and the almighty, I now pronounce you man and wife. What God has joined, let no man put asunder."

Brandon smiled, brushing a lock of unruly dark curls from his forehead and looking at the bride and groom. "You may now kiss the bride."

Teddy leaned in, pressing his lips to Amanda's and feeling like he might take wing right there when Amanda placed a hand at his neck and kissed him back.

"I present to you, Mr. and Mrs. Theodore Lewis!" Brandon shouted, breaking the magic of the kiss.

Teddy grinned, squeezing Amanda's warm hand as he turned to walk back out as man and wife. The loud, riotous cheer that broke the reverence of the ceremony nearly made him take a step back. "Oh my."

"Best, take that little woman out of here," Orville leaned toward Teddy. "Head back to the Hampton House, and we'll get you set for home."

Teddy slipped Amanda's hand into his left one and wrapped his right arm around her waist protectively as they dashed up the aisle and out the door to the whoops and hollers of the men of Needful, Texas.

Amanda cringed, ducking her head as strong hands tried to slap Teddy on the back in congratulations. Was the whole town mad? Didn't they know that you threw rice at a newly-wed couple? Tears pricked at her eyes as Teddy hurried her toward the Hampton House, her long train dragging in the dust of the street, unheeded.

"That was some wedding," Teddy beamed as they finally reached the door of the boardinghouse. "Now, let's get you inside." Strong arms swept Amanda off her feet as Teddy pushed the door open and carried her inside.

"You aren't supposed to carry me over the threshold until we get home," Amanda gasped, grabbing for his collar. "It's for good luck."

"That's why I ain't takin' any chances," Teddy grinned. "I'll carry you over each one, so's we start this marriage out right."

The next hour was a whirlwind as an impromptu wedding supper was organized with what was already on offer at the Hampton House.

Amanda was whisked from person to person on

Teddy's arm while the Hampton men and women organized her things and had them loaded in a wagon.

The young woman was all but dizzy by the time she was handed up onto the hard bench seat of a buckboard wagon, her trunks and bags heaped high behind her.

"All set?" Teddy looked up, meeting her eyes as he stuffed the train of her now bedraggled gown under her feet. "It's time to go home, Mrs. Lewis."

Amanda's eyes grew wide at the man's words, and she started to shake as the reality of her rash decision struck home. She was a married woman. She had married a virtual stranger and was now headed to his humble abode as a wife.

Her mind drifted to the conversation she'd had with Ellen a short while ago and her knees went weak. How was she supposed to get through this night? Could she find the strength to give herself to the man who had just settled beside her?

Amanda flicked her eyes toward Mr. Lewis, studying his face as he grinned at her and set the team into motion.

"Just wait till Cap'n Dan finds out I got hitched," the man beamed. "He'll be tickled pink."

Amanda folded her hands in her lap and lifted a

prayer to heaven above. She had made her choice. Now, she had to live with it.

"Is that your horse?" she asked, her voice breaking as she glimpsed the black and white pinto tied to the back of the wagon.

"That's Pepper," Teddy said, his voice full of pride. "One of the best cow ponies ever to set foot in Texas."

Amanda smiled, wondering if she might have a horse of her own at some point. She didn't even know what Mr. Lewis's situation was other than he worked for one of the biggest ranches in the area.

Silence engulfed the wagon as the team trotted toward the ranch, and Teddy shifted, wondering if his new bride was having second thoughts.

"Amanda?" Teddy's voice was gentle and pulled her from her thoughts. "You know it's my duty to protect and care for you. If you don't feel right about anything, you tell me."

Amanda looked up, meeting his serious eyes. "Thank you, Mr. Lewis," she smiled. "I believe I'm a little overwhelmed by everything, that's all."

"Teddy," the young man said, squeezing her hand. "Call me, Teddy."

Amanda felt her jaw go slack as his name seemed to wrap her in a strange sense of awe. "Teddy," she tried, but the name stumbled on her tongue. "I've never used a man's Christian name before. It feels strange." For several moments she studied the man she had married pondering her discomfort with the diminutive of his name. "May I call you, Theo?"

Teddy straightened as his name tripped off her lips, the sound bringing with it a sense of responsibility and manliness. "I think I'd like that," he agreed. "It has a nice ring."

Amanda smiled, feeling more comfortable with the formality of Mr. Lewis's name. Surely if she could get through this night, everything would fall into place come morning.

Teddy scooped his new bride out of the wagon as he pulled up to the little cabin he called home, and boldly carried her across the threshold. He liked the way the little woman felt in his arms, and he longed to kiss her again.

Stepping through the door of his private domain, he lowered his lips, kissing her softly. "Welcome home, Mrs. Lewis," he grinned. "Your castle awaits."

Amanda laughed despite the flutter of nerves in her belly. The place was no palace, but it seemed sturdy enough. Her eyes fell on the three-quarter bed by the fireplace and heat raced to her cheeks. "I think you can put me down now," she whispered.

Teddy carefully lowered Amanda to the floor, her delicate white boots clicking on the hardwood. "I know it ain't much," he said, "but in time, we can add on. The cattle business is good, and Dan pays fair wages. I'll fetch your things while you make yourself ta home."

Amanda turned slowly, taking in the simple building. It had a fireplace, a bed, a small cupboard, a bureau, and one solitary window. A washbasin sat by the door and a bucket in the far corner. Primitive was the word she would have used to describe the cabin.

"What do you think?" Teddy asked, carrying a heavy trunk inside and placing it in a corner.

"You don't have a kitchen?"

"No, but I can order a stove from the Sears and Roebuck catalog if you'd like. I take all of my meals at the big house, so I never considered the need for a kitchen or any such thing." Teddy scratched his head under his hat then turned to retrieve another trunk from the wagon.

Amanda felt her shoulders sag as Theo's words sank in. She wouldn't have to cook, at least not yet. They could eat at the main house for a while. Perhaps the pretty Rosa would teach her to cook, and in time, she would be a proper country wife.

"How much did you bring with you?" Teddy asked, carrying another trunk into the cabin, his knees bent against the strain.

"Only what I thought I'd need," Amanda replied. "I can send for the rest later."

"The rest?" Teddy stood, rubbing his spine. "I didn't know women needed so much."

Amanda studied her shoes, uncertain of what to say. "I'm sure I can adjust to much less."

Teddy felt like a heel, he hadn't meant to make his young bride feel ashamed. He was genuinely shocked at the amount of baggage that had accompanied her.

"I didn't mean nothin' by it," he said, stepping up and lifting her chin. "This is your home, and I want you to feel comfortable in it."

Amanda met his eyes, suddenly hoping he would kiss her again, and that is exactly what he did.

The kiss seemed to linger on Amanda's lips long after Theo left to retrieve another trunk. His gentle touch and warm embrace had been welcome, and she found herself relaxing as she moved around the small house, becoming familiar with her new home.

"That's the last one," Teddy finally said as he stacked the smallest trunk on a larger one. "I'll fetch your bags and then take the wagon up to the barn. We can return it tomorrow when we go to church."

"We'll go back to town tomorrow?" Amanda blushed, wondering what the reception would be.

"Sure, Dan gives us as much of the Sabbath off as is possible on a big place like this. A few punchers don't attend, and they're happy to look after things while the rest of us go to town."

Teddy walked back outside, hefting the last few bags and setting them by the door. He couldn't believe he was finally married, and it was all he could do to stop his giddy heart from making him kiss Amanda senseless. He could tell she was nervous, and having been raised in a very proper way, he wondered what their wedding night would be like.

"You'll just have to be patient," he reminded himself as he climbed into the buckboard and drove to the barn.

"You're back late," Dan grinned as Teddy started to unhitch the team. "What'd you need a wagon for." The rancher's eyes flickered toward Teddy's house as a grin spread across his rugged face.

"To bring my new bride home," Teddy said, puffing out his chest.

"Bride!" Dan's eyes grew wide. "You got hitched?"

"Yes." Teddy crossed his arms over his chest, meeting Dan's gaze. "She was willing to have me, and I wanted to keep her from the minute I saw her."

Dan reached out a hand. "Congratulations, Teddy," he drawled. "You bring your new bride to the house tomorrow, but be prepared for an earful from Rosa. She will not be well pleased to have missed another Needful wedding."

Teddy nodded, hearing the truth in his boss's words. "Maybe you can smooth the way for me," he suggested.

"I'll do what I can," Dan agreed, thumping Teddy on the shoulder. "I think the next few days around here are going to be interesting. You plan on going to church tomorrow?"

"Yes, Amanda and I can return the wagon tomorrow."

"And how exactly will your blushing bride get

home again once you turn the wagon over?" Dan's blue eyes twinkled merrily as he teased his young friend.

"I hadn't thought of that. Do you reckon I'll need to buy a wagon of my own?"

Dan shook his head. "She can ride back with Rosa and Christina," Dan said. "I'll ride in on my own."

Teddy let a breath he had been holding out with a grin. "Thanks, Dan. I guess I wasn't thinking ahead past the wedding."

"It takes some time to adjust to married life," Dan mused. "Be patient."

"Daniel," Rosa's voice called from the front porch. "Christina is asking for you."

A bright smile flashed across Dan's face as he turned toward his house that had finally become a home. "I'm coming darlin'," he drawled, giving Teddy a wink.

***

Amanda paced the small house, looking at the simple furnishings and rustic appointments. There was a door at both ends of the little house and she walked to the back peering out at the necessary set beside a stunted tree.

Teddy had been gone for what seemed ages, and she was already starting to fret, a thousand worries flashing through her brain in seconds. What if Theo changed his mind? What if he decided she wasn't good wife material? He would be sorely disappointed in her skills as a wife once he got to know her.

The sound of humming caught Amanda's attention and she hurried to the door to see her new husband traipsing toward her in the last light of the day.

"I was starting to worry," she admitted. "You were gone for a long time."

"I had to put the horses up, and then Dan stopped to congratulate us on our marriage." He smiled, taking her arm and walking her back into the house.

Amanda relaxed at Theo's gentle touch. "I'll build us a fire," he said, pushing the door closed. "Nights out here can grow cool even after the heat of the day."

Amanda gazed around the room once more. "Theo," she started as Teddy moved to the fireplace, striking a match to the kindling laid in a neat pile. "Where am I to change?"

Teddy looked over his shoulder, his eyes running over the delicate dress his little wife wore.

"Here, of course," he replied.

"But there's no privacy screen or room."

Understanding hit Teddy and he nodded. "I'll step outside if that will help," he said. "Maybe in time..." he didn't finish his sentence as the flame caught and he rose, catching the flash of embarrassment in her pale eyes.

"Thank you," she breathed.

Teddy strode toward the door giving his blushing bride her privacy, closing the door behind him with a sigh.

Amanda sucked in a deep breath. She was surprised that Theo had been willing to step out while she changed. She would just slip into her nightdress and wrap.

Reaching behind her, Amanda started on the buttons at her back, but the tiny mother of pearl disks and simple loops that held her dress closed wouldn't budge. Her arms burned as again and again, she tried to get out of the elegant dress and hot tears began to fall.

"Theo!" she finally called in embarrassed exasperation. "I need your help."

Teddy dashed into the house. "What's wrong?" he asked, looking around.

"I can't..." Amanda sniffed, pointing at the buttons down her back.

Teddy grinned. Perhaps his young wife would need to get over her shyness sooner rather than later, he thought as his fingers trembled on the first button of the beautiful dress.

Chapter 8

Teddy took Amanda's hand, kissing it softly as they walked toward the door. Today would be their first real day as husband and wife, and he couldn't wait to sit with the pretty woman in church.

He had worried, the night before that she wasn't ready to be his wife in every way, but together they had gotten through those first awkward moments of intimacy, and he felt more connected to Amanda than ever before.

"You look lovely," Teddy grinned, admiring the violet dress his new wife wore. "You sure have a powerful number of pretty things."

Amanda blushed, tying the ribbon of her matching bonnet. Teddy had been accommodating all morning and had even buttoned her dress. Now she was hungry and thinking of nothing more than breakfast.

"You're sure Rosa won't mind if we join everyone for breakfast?"

"No, she'll expect us. Besides, this way you'll get to meet the crew, and they'll keep an eye out for you. I'm sure in no time you'll be fast friends with Rosa and little Christina. We'd better hurry though, we're already running late."

"Late?" Amanda gaped, the sun had barely reached the top of the low hills as a half globe, and she was dressed and ready to leave.

Teddy placed his hand at the young woman's back and opened the door, ushering her out into the light of a new day.

"Theo-dore!" Rosa spat as Teddy walked into the main house. "How come you not tell us that you are getting married?" The fiery woman shook the spatula she had been flipping pancakes with at Teddy. "We could have made a big party."

"I didn't know," Teddy pleaded. "We just kind of decided, and it happened."

"With half the town turnin' out to watch," Cookie snapped as he walked an empty platter from the table.

Amanda shrank back from the old man, but Teddy's soft laugh in her ear steadied her. "Don't worry, Cookie's bark is far worse than his bite."

"Come, eat," Rosa said, carrying the platter of pancakes to the waiting cowhands. "Cookie will bring more bacon."

Amanda took the seat that Theo offered, gazing around her at the curious faces of the other men. She recognized Mayor Dan, from her first encounter on the ranch, but everyone else was strangers.

"I'd like you all to meet my wife, Amanda." Teddy beamed with pride. "Amanda, this here is Rosa, and that's little Christina, you met them before." He blushed, pointing at the little girl sitting next to Dan in a tall, highchair.

The men around the table each greeted Amanda putting her more at ease, though she was sure she would never remember their names. She had thought this initial meeting would be awkward, but so far, everyone seemed happy to see her there.

"Your dress is beautiful," Rosa said, taking a seat and offering a smile. "Come now, we eat."

An hour later, Amanda settled on the seat of the buckboard with Theodore, feeling nervous but happy. So far, this married life wasn't too bad, and she seemed to be handling each challenge well enough.

Theo squeezed her hand as they set out, and she scooted a little closer to him.

"We'll drop the buckboard off at the livery this

morning," Teddy spoke. "You'll ride back with Rosa and Christina."

"What about you?" Amanda blanched. "Aren't you coming home?"

"I'll ride Pepper." He turned slightly to look at his placid pony trotting behind the wagon. "Can you ride?"

"Yes, of course." Amanda turned, looking at the horse then down at her dress. It was not the kind of thing one wore riding.

"I don't mean today, but if you're of a mind to ride sometime, I can organize a quiet horse for you. I don't want you to feel like you're stuck at home while I'm out workin' all the time."

"I don't have a saddle," Amanda protested.

"Well, we'll see what we can do about that. Dan has plenty of saddles. I'm sure one of them will suit."

Amanda felt her cheeks flame, she didn't want to be a problem for Theodore, but she needed to explain. "I ride sidesaddle." The words tumbled out and Amanda dropped her eyes as Theo's brows rose.

"Oh, of course." Teddy sat in silence for several moments, contemplating the issue. "I'll talk to

Darwin when I drop off the wagon," he finally said. "I don't know if he has a sidesaddle, but maybe he can help me get one."

Amanda relaxed a little at Theo's words. The thought of riding astride was simply too indecent to consider. "I would appreciate that."

"If you need anything else while I'm workin', you can always walk up to the house and ask Rosa. She goes to town fairly often, and you can always ride along."

Though quaint, Amanda enjoyed the church service in Needful and was surprised at the number of people who took the time to greet and congratulate her and Theo. It would be a long time before she remembered all of the names of the people who stopped to shake her hand, but they made her feel welcome.

"I see you survived your first night as a wife," Ellen teased, making Amanda's face flush. "Teddy's a good man," the other woman grinned. "You chose well."

Teddy smiled, shaking hands with friends and acquaintances as they greeted him, but his face froze when the saloon owner paused, his eyes roaming over Amanda critically.

"If I'd known you were such a pretty thing," Mr. Alder spoke, a hard glint in his eye, "I'd have come callin' myself. Why, with the money I make in the saloon, you'd have lived the kind of life a lady like yourself deserves."

Teddy stepped closer to Amanda, wrapping an arm around her possessively. "I'm not sure life as the wife of a saloon owner is what one might call fit for a lady."

Mr. Alder chuckled, walking away with a quick retort. "If you ever get tired of this country bumpkin, you come see me." His dark eyes lit on Amanda again, and she sank into Teddy's embrace, offering a haughty look for the rude man.

"I'm starting to think I was fortunate to meet you first," Amanda admitted looking at Theo. "Now, may we go home?"

Teddy walked Amanda to the waiting wagon as Dan handed him Pepper's reins. He still couldn't believe, after what he had done upon Amanda's arrival, that she had consented to marry him. Perhaps he was just the best pick of what was available, but he knew if he worked hard, he could indeed win her heart.

Chapter 9

Monday morning broke, cool and misty as the first watery glint of light touched the window of the tiny cabin and Teddy rolled out of bed.

"Is it time to get up?" Amanda blinked, bleary-eyed into the darkness.

"You go on and sleep if you want to," Teddy leaned over, placing a soft kiss on her forehead. "I've got to get to the house and start chores."

Amanda sat up, squinting at the faint line of light along the horizon through the blank window. "It's still dark."

Teddy grinned. "That's life on a ranch, darlin'. Up at the crack of dawn, long days in the saddle, and plenty to do."

"What am I to do while you're gone?" Amanda felt her stomach knot.

"Whatever you'd like. You just trundle on up to the house when you're ready. I'll ask Rosa to hold a plate for ya, and you two can get to know each other."

Amanda nodded, wondering what she and the lovely Mexican woman would ever find to talk about. Rosa was bold, confident, and full of spunk, while Amanda was timid, fretful, and confused.

"I'll come with you," she said, throwing the blankets off and climbing from the depths of the warm bed. "I don't think I'd like to be here alone in the dark. What if one of those horrid cows turns up?"

Teddy pulled Amanda into his arms, kissing her sweetly. He loved the way she felt tucked up next to him, but he was trying to take his time and let her adjust to married life. "Suit yourself," he grinned. "Maybe Dan should think about putting up a fence around the main property to keep the cattle from wandering through the place, not that they tend to," he added quickly at Amanda's horrified expression.

The noise and bustle of the main house washed over Amanda upon entry, in a disorienting wave as voices mingled in a cacophony. Men she had never seen before straddled chairs as the old cook and Rosa placed stacks of food before them.

"Mornin'," Teddy offered, striding to the table and pulling out a chair for Amanda as she reluctantly followed. "What's on the schedule for the day?"

"The usual," Cookie grumbled. "Eat up so's we can get it done before the cows come home."

The whole table erupted in laughter, making Amanda flinch. She suddenly felt completely out of place with the rowdy cowhands.

Rosa brought a tray of biscuits, taking her seat at the end of the long table and smiling at Amanda. "You eat," she grinned. "You are too skinny for a rancher's wife."

Amanda ducked her head, taking the biscuits and passing them toward Theo, trying to make herself as small as possible as she dodged the scrutiny of the other men.

"Do not listen to these men," Rosa said, eyeing Amanda's fresh floral print dress. "They will talk too much. Today you will stay with Christina and me. I will like having another woman around to help with the work."

Amanda blanched. What could she do to help Rosa? She was singularly ill-equipped to work on a ranch. Perhaps she had married too quickly, and Teddy had not been the best choice. How could a girl from Virginia, who had barely even lifted a finger to serve herself, fit in on a hard-working ranch?

Teddy looked up, trying to catch Rosa's eye, but Dan's wife was busy fixing a plate for her little girl. He wanted to let Rosa know that Amanda might need some time to settle into life on a ranch. He didn't care if Amanda did all of the usual wifely things, he liked her just the way she was.

In a matter of minutes, the food was finished and the men rose to their feet, preparing for the start of a long day.

"I'll try to get back to the ranch for lunch," Teddy whispered, pecking Amanda on the cheek. "Just tell Rosa if you need anything."

Amanda looked up, her luminous blue eyes huge, but she didn't say anything. Finishing her breakfast, the young woman looked toward Rosa feeling completely useless. "Can I help?" The words were a bare whisper.

Rosa wiped Christina's little face, leaning in and kissing the dark-eyed child. "Come, we will clean."

Amanda pulled her chair back from the table, looking down at the dirty plates and wondering where to start. "What do I do?" she asked, hanging her head in shame.

Rosa lifted Christina from her chair, placing the girl on the floor and smoothing her dress.

"You have never washed dishes?" Rosa asked,

starting to gather the dirty plates and cups. "You take," she nodded toward the rest of the dishes on the table.

Amanda gathered a few dishes together, following Rosa to the kitchen and watching as the other woman scraped any leavings into a bucket.

"You will learn," Rosa grinned. "You are not the first Needful bride who is new to this life."

Amanda looked up, relieved at the smile on Rosa's lips. Had other women come to Needful without any skills?

***

Amanda helped Rosa lay out sliced bread, cheese, and meat on a sideboard for lunch, then washed her hands and stepped out the door. She would take some of the offerings to the cabin and hope that Theo would join her. At the moment, she was too tired to think further than that, and her hands were raw from washing dishes.

She had never worked so hard in her life as she had helping Rosa clear the remains of breakfast from the table.

Cringing as the sun blasted down on her head, Amanda realized she had forgotten her bonnet but pressed on to her new home wanting nothing more than to sit down and put her feet up.

The sound of a cow bawling somewhere in the distance made Amanda hurry toward her new home, dodging through the door and closing it quickly behind her.

With a sigh of relief, the young woman walked to one of her trunks and began rummaging through it, laughing when she found the small jar of hand cream. Sinking to the floor, disregarding the dust collecting on her dress, Amanda smeared the cream onto her chaffed hands. "How do women do this every day?" The words echoed into the empty house.

Sagging against the trunk, Amanda leaned back against it closing her eyes as she stretched tired limbs. Rosa wasn't much bigger than Amanda, yet she had worked tirelessly, washing, drying, and putting dishes on a shelf. She had even scrubbed the table and started a massive batch of bread.

"I'm useless," Amanda sniffed tears pricking behind her eyes. "Why did I ever think I could do this?"

Pulling a handkerchief from her sleeve, she dabbed at her eyes, her arms dropping to her lap once more as she quivered with fatigue.

***

AMANDA

Teddy touched heels to Pepper's flanks, letting the horse stretch out for a good run home. He had promised he would join Amanda for lunch, and he smiled, thinking of seeing his pretty wife.

The ranch came into view and Teddy, eased back in the saddle letting Pepper slow. He didn't need everyone on the ranch to see how much he liked his new wife.

Pulling up to the ranch house, Teddy tied Pepper to the hitching post and strolled into the house.

"You back already?" Cookie chuckled as Teddy walked through the door. "Seems like your little woman went home."

"Is something wrong?" Teddy gazed around him, worried that something had happened between Amanda and Rosa? Teddy knew that Rosa could have a sharp tongue and Amanda seemed timid at best. "I'll check on her," he said casually, walking back outside and breaking into a trot as soon as he was out of sight.

Teddy opened the door, hesitating when he saw Amanda sitting against her trunk, her eyes closed. A smile flickered across his face and he hurried to her side, leaning in to place a kiss on her cheek.

"Ahh!" Amanda jerked with a scream, balking as

Teddy tugged at her hand.

"Easy, there," Teddy soothed. "I didn't mean to scare you."

Amanda patted her chest, her breathing slowing once more. "I'm sorry I must have fallen asleep."

Teddy stood, pulling her along with him. "It's been a long day for you."

"Oh, you came home for lunch," Amanda's eyes grew wide. "I brought food for you." Releasing his hand, she hurried to the trunk where she had placed the covered plate.

"What about you, did you already eat?"

Amanda stared at Teddy for a few moments rubbing her hands. "I didn't think."

Teddy's smile was warm as he pulled the old bench toward the trunk, helping her to sit. "You sit," I'll be right back."

Amanda lifted a tiny piece of cheese, nibbling on it only to discover that she was famished.

The door opened again and Teddy returned, shoving the door closed with a foot and walking toward her, his hands full of teapot and cups.

"You don't drink tea," Amanda blinked.

AMANDA

"No, but you do," Teddy grinned pleased with himself. He knew it would take time for his sweet bride to adjust to her new life, but he didn't care. He hadn't married a handmaiden to work for him. He wanted a companion and a friend.

Amanda blushed, weariness bringing tears to her eyes. "Thank you."

Teddy separated the food on the plate, making sure that Amanda had enough to eat.

Finding her manners, Amanda poured the tea. There was no cream or sugar, so she sipped the hot brew black. The first sip washed the dryness from her throat, and the second imbued her with a hint of energy.

"Better?" Teddy asked, stacking meat and cheese between two pieces of bread. "You have to eat proper when you're workin' on a ranch."

Amanda gazed into her teacup, catching a glimpse of her hands that still appeared red from the hot water used to scrub the plates clean.

"I'm so useless," Amanda sighed. "I don't know how Rosa does this every day."

Teddy chuckled, taking a huge bite of his sandwich. "She's been working her whole life. She grew into it."

Amanda sagged, "I'll never fit in."

"Don't worry, darlin'," Teddy grinned around his sandwich. "You're new. I was new once too."

Amanda's eyes fluttered, shocked at her husband's poor manners, but intrigued by his words. Taking a piece of bread, she pulled off a piece eating it in a delicate bite.

"When Cap'n Dan come here, I didn't know a thing about cows. To tell the truth, they scared me." Teddy washed down his bite with a swig of bitter tea. "Now look at me. I'm a top hand and someone the Captain depends on."

Amanda smiled, letting Theo's words sink in, giving her hope.

"Don't be too hard on yourself," Teddy continued. "Just take it a day at a time. If you're tired, tell Rosa and come on home. She and Cookie can manage just fine on their own."

Teddy reached out, patting Amanda's knee. "My mother used to tell me a story about a tortoise and a hare. It seems they were challenged to a race and the hare was so confident he could beat that old tortoise he done took a nap." Teddy's laugh was bright, though his eyes were sad. "That slow, steady, tortoise just kept going till he got to the finish line."

"Are you calling me a tortoise?" Amanda grinned, taking Theo's point.

"Darlin', just take your time and you'll get there in the end."

Amanda leaned over, pecking Teddy on the cheek. He was being kind, and she would accept it as that.

Chapter 10

The rest of the week seemed to blur and Amanda tried her best to keep up with the work Rosa had for her, but it was so grueling she often returned home at noon whether Theo was going to be there or not.

With each day on the ranch, Amanda noticed new things, moments of beauty in wildflowers thriving in the dusty earth, or a new foal frolicking with its mother in a field. Her favorite afternoon past time was watching the birds.

With plentiful water close at hand, the birds seemed to congregate in the trees around her new home, their cheerful song lifting her spirits. She was weary. Her hands were raw and she felt like a complete failure as a wife, but still, she tried.

Amanda placed the food items on the trunk where she and Theodore had been enjoying their afternoon repast then flopped down onto the bed. If she could just close her eyes for a few minutes, she would feel better.

***

Teddy walked into his cabin as the afternoon sun was slipping toward the western horizon. It had been a long day, and he had expected to see Amanda at the supper table. When Rosa explained that Amanda had gone home shortly after lunch, his heart lurched as worry and fear clutched at it.

Perhaps he hadn't known the young woman long, but the joy of coming home to her every day, brought was inexplicable.

"Please, Lord, let her be all right," he whispered as he rushed home and pushed open the door, sucking in a relieved breath when he saw his wife asleep in their bed.

Teddy looked around the cabin, checking that nothing else could be wrong, and spotted the plate of cold meat and cheese on the trunk. Various items of clothing were scattered throughout the house and one of Amanda's trunks stood open, frilly things spilling onto the floor.

Walking to the bed, Teddy squatted, looking into Amanda's sleeping face. She looked so peaceful, he didn't want to disturb her, but the dark circles under her eyes worried him.

Gently, he brushed a lock of brown hair from her brow, smiling when her blue eyes fluttered open.

"Theo," Amanda sighed, pushing herself upright and rubbing her eyes. "You came home for lunch."

"Darlin', it's time for supper," Teddy said. "Have you been asleep all afternoon?"

"I'm so sorry." Amanda blushed, dropping her eyes as tears appeared. "I didn't mean to sleep. I was just so tired."

Teddy grasped Amanda's hands in his, scowling when she flinched. "Your hands?" he Iquestioned. "They're nigh unto raw."

"I'm afraid I'm not used to washing things myself." Amanda tried to hide her hands, but Teddy held them gently in his. "I've been putting cream on them, but it doesn't seem to help."

Teddy lifted one of her hands, examining it. The delicate skin was chafed and red. "I'll get you something for it," he smiled. "You just sit here a minute."

"But what about supper?"

"Don't you worry about supper," Teddy cast a reassuring smile over his shoulder. "I'll see to that."

Amanda watched as Theo hurried from the house, hanging her head in shame. She had been a fool to come here as a bride. She hadn't been raised to this kind of life, and she was sure she was a terrible disappointment to her husband and his friends. Hot tears splashed onto her hands, stinging the roughened skin, and the tears fell faster.

"I'm just tired," the young woman chided herself. "I'll be alright after some food and a good night's sleep."

Nearly half an hour passed before Teddy returned, and Amanda worried that he had gone to supper without her, seeking a chance to complain about her performance with his friends. Her heart squeezed at the thought. Perhaps she didn't know Teddy yet, but he seemed such a gentle soul, and she thought he liked her. Amanda felt terrible for being a disappointment.

A bright smile broke across her face as Teddy pushed open the door carrying a heavily laden tray to the trunk and setting it there. A moment later, he was kneeling before her again, unscrewing the lid of a small jar of dark ointment.

"It doesn't smell very good," Amanda said as Teddy began applying the salve to her hands.

"But how does it feel?"

Amanda pulled her hands back, rubbing the dark, acrid smelling substance into her hands and sighing as the cracked skin drank it in. "It feels much better."

Teddy smiled. "You put your gloves on over that and then we'll eat. You don't want to have to smell that while you're enjoying your dinner."

Taking Amanda's arm, he helped her to the table and settled her on the cowhide covered bench. She looked tired and frail sitting on the hard surface, surrounded by the rustic composition of his home. Perhaps Olive had been right and Amanda deserved better than him. She should have been a gentleman's wife, living a life of luxury and ease, not working her fingers to the bone on a ranch.

Teddy dropped his head in shame at his selfishness, but he knew he was already growing to love his wife. She was innocent, sweet, and determined, though somewhat lost when it came to homemaking. He gazed around at the disheveled cabin then looked back to her.

"Let me help," he said, taking a plate and filling it with meat, rice, and beans. "I know it's not fancy, but it will fill your belly and put some color back into your cheeks."

"Thank you for being so kind," Amanda sniffed, taking the plate from him. "I'm sorry I'm so useless."

Teddy took the plate, placing it back on the trunk as he pulled his young wife into his arms, letting her tears soak into his collar as she wept out her despair. If only he could think of a way to make her understand how special she was.

"Are you feeling better?" Teddy asked once they had finished the meal. It had taken some coaxing, but he had convinced Amanda she would feel better with a full belly.

"Yes. Thank you." Amanda looked up, meeting Theo's eyes. "I guess I was just tired and hungry."

"I'll tell you what," Teddy grinned, "how about we go to town tomorrow. We can have dinner at the Hampton House, and you can see your friends. Dan can do without me for a day."

Amanda's eyes sparkled with delight. "Are you sure?"

"I'm sure," Teddy grinned, seeing how the idea had cheered her. "I'll talk to Dan tonight, and we can go tomorrow."

Amanda looked down at her dress, now stained from working in the main house with Rosa. She should probably look into more practical clothing for everyday use.

"Thank you," Amanda's voice was soft. "It would be nice to see Olive and the rest of the Hamptons. They were very kind to me while I was there."

Teddy's grin brightened. "I'll tell you what, you pack a bag, and we'll stay at the boarding house for the night and go to church on Sunday. We can buy a picnic from Olive and make a day of it."

"But that will be expensive." Amanda looked up at the simple house around her, surprised when Theo's face darkened.

"I can afford to take my wife to town," he growled, standing to his feet and collecting the dishes. "I ain't some wet behind the ears boy who doesn't know enough to save his pay."

Amanda gaped as Theodore loaded the tray with the dishes and stormed from the house. Still stunned by Theo's behavior, Amanda rose and began picking up the items of clothing scattered about the house. She had always had someone to help her at home. A maid to clean and a girl to help her dress and care for her clothing.

Bundling a dress in her arms, she walked to her trunk, longing for someplace to hang her garments for easy access. How would she ever adapt to this life? What had she said that upset Theodore so? Somewhere between stepping onto the train that brought her to Texas, and now, life had become very complicated. Amanda understood how to make her way in the social rounds of her Virginia home, but Texas was like being in a foreign country where she didn't know the language, rules, or etiquette.

Teddy returned as Amanda was placing two of her best dresses into a bag. She wanted to go to town, but she didn't want to overtax her new husband. She needed to learn how to carry her own weight. Theodore had wanted a wife, not a helpless child.

"Good, you're getting ready," Teddy looked over at his wife, feeling awkward at his snappishness from earlier. He wanted Amanda to know that he could care for and provide for her, even if he couldn't afford fancy dresses, a big house, and all the niceties she'd grown up with.

"I've packed a few dresses, and my night things, just the items I'll need," Amanda smiled, looking at the two bags she had filled moments ago.

"You packed one for me, thank you."

"I," Amanda looked between Theo and the bags. "I will." She smiled, trying to put a brighter note on her mistake.

"You need two bags?" Teddy looked at the bags, then at his wife, who smoothed her ruffled dress.

"I can leave one," Amanda sniffed, feeling foolish.

Teddy's shoulders fell. He had upset Amanda

with his ignorance. It wasn't what he had intended, and he moved toward her, placing his hands on her shoulders. "I don't know what a woman needs when she travels," he said, placing a soft kiss on her forehead. "I'll just put my Sunday duds in a bag, don't worry."

A flicker of annoyance shot through Amanda as she pulled away. Theo was patronizing her. Perhaps she wasn't a good wife or efficient in homemaking, but she was not useless. "I'll pack your things."

Teddy scratched his head, wondering what he had done this time. He had been lonely for so long. Sure, he had his friends, the men he had fought and traveled with, but having someone to love had lingered as the desire of his heart for a long time.

Perhaps the wedding was only the beginning of a relationship. Teddy had much to learn about loving a woman and keeping a wife. Running his hands through his hair, he thought about Amanda's agitation. He didn't even know what he had done to upset his pretty bride.

Turning, Teddy strode to the window, gazing out across the slope of the hill leading toward the pools. He wanted to talk to Amanda, to pour out his heart, share his past and his future, but they were so far apart, how would he ever share the darkness in his soul.

Uncertain what else to do, he pulled his mouth organ from his pocket and stepped out onto the porch while Amanda prepared his things.

Pressing the harmonica to his lips, he let a sad, trilling note drift into the afternoon sky. Old sorrows, aching hurts, and days of blood and fear, pooled in his chest escaping with the sad song as he thought.

***

Amanda hustled around the cabin, her temper simmering as she felt like a stupid little girl. She should have thought to pack a bag for Theodore. Gathering her discarded dresses and stuffing them into her trunk. It was inconvenient not having anywhere to hang her things for easy access.

Outside, a sad song drifted toward the oncoming night, and Amanda's heart sagged. There was so much she didn't know about the man she had married. She didn't even know he played the harmonica.

Finishing her work, she stepped out onto the porch, prepared to apologize and explain.

"We can go to the store tomorrow," Teddy spoke, still staring out over the hills. "If you need anything."

Amanda turned, clutching her favorite lavender dress to her bosom. "I was wondering about one thing," Amanda spoke, feeling nervous about asking. She didn't want to be wasteful with Theo's resources, but this item seemed like a necessity, not a convenience.

"Whatever you need," Teddy turned, smiling his encouragement. "You're my wife, and I want to take care of you."

Amanda swallowed hard, meeting his eyes. "I'd like a tub."

Teddy blinked, surprised at the request. The men on the ranch either washed in the spring or used a big tub in the bunkhouse in the winter. He looked down at his sweat and dust-covered clothing. After a day in the saddle, he needed a good wash and would have headed to the spring on Sunday morning.

"We'll see to it," Teddy grinned, walking across the porch and kissing her cheek. "Maybe Darwin will even have found us a sidesaddle as well."

Amanda smiled, relieved at Theo's agreement. Perhaps this weekend trip to town would turn out well after all.

Chapter 11

"Thank you for driving us to town, Rosa," Amanda said as Theodore handed her down from the wagon.

"I am happy to come," Rosa smiled, handing Christina to Teddy. "I needed to come, and it will be nice to see Olive and the family."

Teddy offered a hand to Rosa, but she ignored it, hopping out of the wagon with a flurry of skirts.

"What will you do today?" Rosa asked, looking between the two newlyweds. "You bring horses to come back, but how you will fill your time?"

"I'm looking forward to visiting with the Hampton's," Amanda said. "Tell Olive we'll be along shortly."

Rosa grinned, giving Teddy a wink as she took Christina and headed into the boarding house.

"Is there something you wanted to do before you see Olive?" Teddy looked down at his petite wife, curiously. "Do you need to go to the store?"

"No," Amanda shook her head, gazing up and down the street. "I just wanted a minute to look at Needful. It isn't much, but it feels nice to be back in a town."

Teddy scowled, not liking Amanda's comment. He knew that adjusting to life on a ranch would be difficult, but she was a smart, plucky, young woman and would soon adapt. "You don't like my place?"

"No. I mean, yes. I like it just fine, but I'm used to the hustle of a big city with shops and people. I just need to see that I'm not alone."

Teddy's scowl deepened. "I'm sorry if you're lonely."

Amanda laid a hand on Teddy's arm. She was making a mess of things and knew it. "I'm not lonely," she sighed. "I just need a little connection now and then. I love working with Rosa; she's very patient, and Christina is a joy. I, I guess I just need a little noise now and then."

A group of rowdy cowboys came galloping up the street as Amanda finished speaking and she crowded in close to Theodore who wrapped an arm around her protectively. "Maybe not that much noise," she grinned as the fast riders disappeared out of town.

"Why don't you go in and visit with Olive and the girls. I'll take the horses and wagon to the livery and bring our bags in once I'm done."

"Thank you," Amanda stretched toward Theo, kissing him on the cheek. "I think this is just what I needed." A break from her ineptitude might give her the strength to carry on.

Teddy watched Amanda walk into the boarding house, listening as old friends greeted her. Was he ever going to be enough for the beautiful woman God had dropped in his lap? Something squirmed in his belly, reminding him that he was no one from nowhere. What right did he have to love a girl like Amanda?

Climbing back up into the buckboard, Teddy turned the wagon in the street, driving it and the two horses tied to the back toward the livery. He hoped that this trip to town would bring him closer to his little wife, but now he was worried they would never be on the same page. He was wide-open spaces; she was big towns and shops. Could they ever truly be one?

***

"You look like you've been suckin' lemons," Darwin Rivers greeted, as he ducked out of the big barn smiling at Teddy. "Somethin' on your mind?"

Teddy stepped down from the wagon, letting

Darwin take charge of the horses and harness while he untied Pepper, and a pretty palomino, called Pal, he'd brought for Amanda to ride.

"I don't want to talk about it," he growled, giving the black-haired hostler a hard glare.

"Women troubles," Darwin said, shaking his head. "Only thing that can make a man that surly, is women troubles."

"There's no trouble," Teddy snapped," matching stride with Darwin as they led the horses to the corral. "I just brought Amanda into town for a couple of days to give her a break. She ain't used to the kind of work a woman has to do on a ranch."

Darwin nodded. "She's kind of delicate."

Teddy paused, running the reins of both mounts through his fingers. "She's citified, is all."

"So was Ruth," Darwin smiled, his eyes sparkling with love. "She didn't know nothin' about being a wife, or cookin' or housework."

"Yes, but Ruth wanted an adventure. Your wife is bright, cheerful, and interested in everything. Mine is more a delicate flower."

"Teddy, just because she wasn't raised on a ranch and isn't used to this new life, doesn't mean she can't grow into it. You've only been married a week. You need to give it time."

"You think so?"

"Yes. Give it time, let her get to know you, love you. Love can overcome a heap of troubles."

Teddy felt a smile flash across his face. Darwin's wife, Ruth, had grown up in a fancy house, with pretty things around, and she was content to live in the little house by the big barn. Maybe what the other man was saying was true.

"You think she can love me?"

"She married you, didn't she?" Darwin offered a cheeky grin. "If she didn't want to be married and live in Texas, why did she come?"

"She didn't like her mother's new husband," Teddy stated the fact boldly. "What choice did she have?"

"If her Mama has money, and she wasn't happy here, she could have turned around and lit out on the early stage. She didn't. She chose to stay and to marry you. You must have made some kind of impression on her."

"You think so?"

"Teddy, be patient. Give the girl a chance to adjust to Needful. She'll come around."

Teddy smiled, feeling hope wash through his heart. Time, he could do that.

"Thanks, Dar," he grinned, turning to strip the saddle from Pepper's back. "I'll do my best."

A minute later, Teddy had turned the horses into the corral, grabbed the three bags from the wagon, and headed for the Hampton House and his sweet little bride.

***

"Amanda!" Olive greeted cheerfully as the young woman walked into the boarding house. "It's so good to see you." The older woman's dark eyes examined Amanda as if assessing her well being. "Are you well?"

"Yes, thank you." Amanda's smile was bright and she was thrilled to see her first friends of Needful. "Theodore is putting the horses up."

Olive grinned, no one called Teddy Theodore unless they were upset with him. "Rosa said you and Teddy plan to stay here for the weekend. That will be a treat. How are you finding life on the range?" She smiled again this time, waving down Arabela, "Would you mind bringing us tea, dear?" she asked politely.

"I'll let Ellen know you're here," the stately

young woman replied. "She's due for a break anyway."

Amanda moved to the table where Olive and Rosa were seated, taking a chair and peeling off her gloves.

"Amanda, your hands!" Olive expostulated, grabbing for the girl's reddened hands.

"They're fine," Amanda blushed. "I'm afraid I'm not used to using them the way I need to on the ranch."

"They will get tougher," Rosa stated blandly.

"Theo brought some salve, and it has helped tremendously already."

"Is he taking good care of you?" Olive looked closely at Amanda, demanding an answer.

"Yes, of course." Amanda blushed, worried that Olive thought Theo was mistreating her in some way. "He's very attentive and kind. I think he is worried that I was working too hard, and that's why he wanted to spend the weekend in town."

"It is good," Rosa said. "When I married Dan, we went away on this honey-mooning. It did not go well. It is better to stay here, where you have friends if something happens."

Amanda swallowed hard. So far, she had heard

of a kidnapping, arrested outlaws, a killing, and now this. What was wrong with Needful?

"Don't worry," Ellen arrived with a tray laden with tea and treats. "Needful is a fairly safe town for the wilds of Texas. Sheriff Gaines works hard to make it a better place for women like us all the time. He does have a vested interest after all, with Daliah and Chad depending on him."

Amanda felt herself relax as Ellen joined them pouring tea and handing out cookies. With Ellen, she didn't' feel like she was continually being assessed for her value. The other woman was kind, simple, and straight to the point.

"So how's married life," Ellen teased, shooting Amanda a wicked grin. "Everything I said it would be?"

Amanda blushed bright red but laughed. "There seems to be a good deal of work involved," she added.

"That's why I thought you should have given us more time to find someone who would keep you in the style you have been accustomed to," Olive shot, lifting her cup. It seemed that every time she had a match figured out, the young women did something different.

"But, I like Theodore!"

"Mother, don't go on about it. Amanda has made her choice, and she'll adapt. It doesn't matter who you marry or where you live, there is always an adjustment period."

"That's true," Olive conceded, sipping her tea. "There's Teddy now."

"Mornin', ladies," Teddy greeted, stripping the hat from his head. "It's nice to see you having a good time."

Amanda looked down at her plate, shyly wondering if Theo would want to join them for tea. She couldn't see him sipping tea and swapping gossip with a group of women.

"Darwin found a side saddle for you," Teddy beamed. "I'm gonna put it on Pal, and let her get used to it a bit. Will you be alright here?"

"Yes, thank you," Amanda agreed with relief. "I can't see you sitting in a side-saddle, though."

Teddy chuckled. "I'll put some sacks of feed on the saddle and lead Pal while I ride Pepper. Darwin seems to know what he's doing with the odd contraption, so we'll have an idea how the horse takes to it before you have to mount up."

"Thank you," Amanda grinned at the man. "I'll see you later then."

Teddy returned Amanda's smile, pleased that he had made his wife happy, then spun on his heel and strode back out of the house.

"He does seem to want to make you happy," Olive said, watching the young man leave. "That's got to mean a lot."

"I'm afraid he worries that because he doesn't have a fancy house and loads of money, I'll be unhappy." The words tumbled out of Amanda's mouth and she gasped in surprise. "I shouldn't have said that."

"Why not?" Ellen asked. "If that's what you think, you have a right to speak."

"It is difficult understanding a man at first," Rosa grinned, handing Christina another cookie. "I did not understand Daniel for a very long time."

Amanda looked at Rosa hopefully, but the woman said no more.

"I hope that Theo and I can come to understand each other better. I don't need fancy things," she blushed, "though I do appreciate them and am struggling to fit into this new life, but I had everything back home, and I was not happy."

"Your family does know you're here, don't they?" Olive gave Amanda another look. The girl had indicated that she had gone with her family's blessing, but she knew too well that some girls snuck out to find a new life on their own.

"Yes, of course. Mother wasn't happy, but my new stepfather seemed relieved."

"As long as no one is going to come looking for you and blame me," Olive said wearily. "I think I need to leave this matchmaking up to Peri."

Ellen's giggle was contagious and soon, they were all laughing. It was evident that Olive still believed that what this town needed most were good wives.

"Teddy seems very interested in your well being," Ellen's comment pulled everyone back. "I hope you will enjoy your weekend here together. It will be nice for you to have some time together without any responsibilities."

Amanda nodded, unsure what to say. It would be different spending most of the two days with her husband, without him working and her trying to be of some use around the ranch.

Chapter 12

Amanda spent a lovely couple of hours visiting with Olive and the other Hampton girls when business slacked off. It felt lovely to sit and sip tea with friends, and Amanda felt more at home than she had since her arrival.

Teddy returned around lunchtime as Rosa and Christina were leaving, and seemed delighted at the idea of having a quiet lunch with his wife.

Around them, several men glared, but no one interrupted as the newest couple of Needful enjoyed the excellent food provided by the Hampton House.

"Orville took our bags to one of the rooms," Amanda explained as she tasted the excellent soup. "It was very nice having a chance to visit with Ellen and her family," she added with a smile. She wanted Theo to know how much she appreciated this time and the break from the rigors of a life she knew nothing about.

"How about after lunch we take a walk and head

to the general store?" Teddy asked. "I don't want you fussing about money either. If you need anything, you tell me. If it's too much, I'll put it on layaway for later."

Amanda sat up straighter, amazed at Theo's words. It had always been distasteful to discuss finances in her home. She knew her father had accrued a good deal of wealth over the years, but they seldom discussed it. Her mother simply purchased whatever she wanted. Any whim would do as an excuse for a shopping expedition.

"Thank you," Amanda said, not sure what else she could say. With her new life, there were a few things she wanted, but she didn't want to take too much when she seemed able to give so little

The sun was warm as they left the boarding house dining room and started down the boardwalk. Amanda took Theo's arm, and they strolled slowly along the dusty street as he pointed out more details of the town.

"So, Dan Gaines started the town?" Amanda asked. She had heard so many things about Needful from so many people it was all muddled in her head.

"You could say that. Dan picked this place to build a ranch, and it happened to be close to a trading post. Over the way, there's a mine for Mikolite, and once we settled here, the trader started doing more business, which drew men from there. Then other men came who wanted some land and the town started to grow."

"But it wasn't named until the wagon train with Dan's brother, Spencer, arrived and the Hamptons built their boarding house?"

"That's right," Teddy smiled. "Now it's Needful, Texas, a town to be proud of."

Amanda looked down the dusty street at the few false fronted businesses as the tinkle of a player piano spilled out of the saloon. It didn't seem like much of a town to her, but now it was home. She only hoped it would all turn out well for her. It was apparent from the first moment that they had met that Theodore Lewis wanted her to be his. Amanda hoped that would be enough to overcome their differences.

Teddy ushered Amanda into the store, smiling as they entered, for the first time as husband and wife.

"Hello there, Teddy," William Scripts grinned. "I take it this is the new Mrs."

"William, this is Amanda."

"Mrs. Lewis, it's nice to meet you. What can I do for you today?"

Amanda glanced at Theo, then met the other man's dark eyes. "I was hoping you might have some readymade dresses," she said. "I'm afraid my wardrobe is not well suited to my new responsibilities."

Teddy's eyes grew wide. He appreciated the pretty things his wife wore, but on closer inspection, they were not the best thing for helping Rosa at the ranch house.

"I'm afraid we don't have readymade dresses," Mr. Scripts said, scratching his head of dark hair. "I could ask Alice, and maybe she knows someone who can make you something."

Teddy studied Amanda's disappointed face then took her hand. "Why don't you look at the fabrics you might like while William checks with Mrs. Scripts, that way, you'll have an idea of what's available."

Amanda nodded. "That sounds like a good idea." A moment later, she was perusing the calico and gingham on display, wondering what would best suit her everyday needs.

"Amanda, it's so nice to see you again," Alice Scripts hustled into the store's main room with a smile. "William said you needed some dresses." She looked down at Amanda's fashionable, yet impractical garb. "I take it you don't sew."

Amanda looked up, spotting Theo chatting with Mr. Scripts and shook her head. "I've never needed to," she admitted.

"Well, don't you worry, I'll think of someone who might have the time to do something up nice for you."

The door behind them opened, and a blonde woman in a bright green dress walked into the store.

"Hello, Beth," Mrs. Scripts greeted. "Have you met Amanda?"

"Only in passing," the pretty woman smiled, her green eyes bright. "At the wedding as a matter of fact," she added. "It's nice to see you again."

Amanda nodded in acknowledgment.

"Amanda is looking for someone to do some sewing for her," Alice continued. "Do you know of anyone who might want to pick up a little ready cash for the work?"

Beth's eyes widened. "As a matter of fact, I'd be willing to do it," she said, looking at Amanda hopefully. "I've always made my dresses." She furled her skirt lightly, highlighting the workmanship.

"That does look comfortable," Amanda said,

looking at the simple lines and lack of bustle on the practical dress.

"It's also cool in this heat," Beth grinned.

***

"You're a lucky man," William said, leaning on the counter and watching the women examining fabric. "She's a pretty thing and interested in fitting in here in Needful."

"Thanks," Teddy grinned. "She is kind of special. I think she worries that she isn't homey enough, but I knew that when I told her I wanted to wed. Out at the ranch, most things are taken care of. Rosa and Cookie take care of the food, the bunkhouse has all the comforts of home, and since we're out on the range most of the day, I never thought I needed much else."

"Now, you want to give her the world."

Teddy nodded. "I'm not sure she's suited for this kind of life, she's delicate like."

"She'll grow into it," William said. "Mark my words."

Teddy prayed that the other man was right and that Amanda would be happy in their simple home. He had big dreams and ideas for building his little house into a larger home when the time was right. "That reminds me," he said, looking up at the tall storekeeper. "I need a tub."

By the time Amanda and Teddy had finished their shopping, Rosa had arrived with the wagon for her supplies, collecting the few items that needed to be delivered to the ranch.

"Thank you for everything," Amanda smiled as she and Teddy bid farewell to Rosa and the others. "Now, what shall we do?"

"I thought you might want to try riding Pal around the corral a bit to see how she takes to the saddle. She did right good with the sacks, but that's different than a regular rider."

"Of course. I'll go and change now."

"Change?" Teddy looked down at the woman's pale blue dress. "What do ya need to change for?"

"I need my riding clothes, of course." Amanda smiled again as if the answer was obvious.

"Oh," Teddy stuttered, seeing the gulf between him and his wife widen. He surely wasn't the man to be married to a lady like Amanda.

"I'll ask Ellen to help and be right down," Amanda said, touching his arm as they reached the boarding house. "I'll be out as quickly as possible."

"I'll be ready," Theo growled, stomping off toward the corner of the Hampton House and the big livery barn behind.

Ellen was as excited as Amanda about the new dresses and they chatted as she helped her friend into a dark green riding habit. "You'll feel more at home in one of the new dresses," she said. "I wish I had been there to see what you chose. Alice keeps some pretty fabrics on hand. You never know when a new bride will arrive and want a dress."

Amanda laughed, looking down at her outfit. It did seem rather much for the tiny town of Needful, but she had been raised in such a way that she couldn't imagine wearing anything else when riding.

"Do you think I'm silly changing into my riding garb?" she asked, meeting Ellen's eyes.

"No, if that's what you're comfortable in, I think it's best. You don't want to feel awkward sitting on a horse that isn't used to a side saddle."

"Do you ride?" Amanda asked. "Perhaps you'd come out with me one day."

"No, I'm too busy here at the Hampton House, not to mention with the children. It's not too bad when they're at school with Mr. Ben, but then there's homework and such to be done."

Amanda squeezed, Ellen's hand, thankful for

such a friend. "Perhaps one day, I'll have a child, and you can help me learn how to be a mother."

Ellen's sharp bark of laughter filled the room, startling Amanda. "Honey, it doesn't matter what training you have in being a mother, every child is different. I can teach you to make diapers, though," she added with a wink.

Chapter 13

Amanda settled herself into the familiar arms of her new saddle and took the reins from Theo with a smile. It felt nice to be sitting a horse again. She thought of her own fine gelding back home in Virginia and for a moment, homesickness swept over her.

"Is everything all right?" Teddy looked up with worried eyes.

"I'm fine," Amanda assured. "It's just been a while since I've ridden, and it feels nice to sit a horse again."

Teddy's grin was bright. "How about you take it nice and slow around the yard and see how Pal does. She's a quiet little thing, and I don't imagine you'll have any trouble.

Amanda nodded, gathering the reins and tapping the horse with her heel. Pal stepped to the side a few paces and then stopped.

"That's not right," Amanda said. "How do you

make her go forward?"

"With my heels or a click of my tongue," Teddy replied.

Amanda adjusted her seat again, pressing her heel into the horse's side and clicking. This time the palomino moved forward, but her hips swung to the side.

"She's used to being guided with heels," Teddy said, scratching his head. "We need her to understand what forward means." Reaching out, he took the bridle and set the horse straight again. "Do it again, and this time I'll pull her forward a bit."

Amanda did as he said, and this time Pal stepped out following him quickly, even as her side quivered under Amanda's heel.

"She'll get the hang of it."

After several false starts, the little mare did indeed figure out what was being asked, and once Amanda adjusted to neck reining instead of driving the horse, they settled into a leisurely amble about the yard.

"You look right pretty sitting up there," Teddy offered. Amanda seemed confident on a horse, and he realized that this, at least, was something they both had in common.

He watched, proud of Amanda's calm demeanor and easy patience as the horse learned new cues, and smiled when she rode toward him with a grin.

"Can we go for a short ride?" Amanda asked, her blue eyes bright with hope.

"Sure," Teddy agreed. "I'll get Pepper while you ride around a bit more and get the feel of how Pal moves."

In no time, he had his black and white pinto saddled and moved into step with Amanda steering them toward the main street of the town.

"You seem comfortable on horseback," Teddy commented as they moved along the street toward the other side of town.

"I've been riding since I was just a little girl," Amanda replied. "I love horses. Back home, we used to do fox hunting on occasion, though father usually let the fox go unless it had been raiding the hen house. We had long rides in the spring and fall, with lavish picnics, or fun outings."

Teddy nodded, trying to imagine the life Amanda had left behind. Did she miss it? Would she come to resent his simple living and simpler ways?

Several passers-by paused to smile and wave at Teddy and Amanda as they rode by, and his heart swelled with pride for his wife. Perhaps she wasn't a good homemaker, but she had her own skills, education, and ways.

"Mighty fine lookin' woman you got there, Teddy." Mr. Alder drawled as he stepped out of his saloon, drying his hand on a heavy white apron tied around his stout middle. "A fine lady," he added, bowing slightly.

"Mr. Alder," Teddy replied tersely. "My wife and I are out for a ride."

"I can see that," the man laughed. "Seems a lady like that should be sitting a better horse than the one you gave her."

"Ma'am, if you ever get tired of this country bumpkin, you come on over and see me," the man's grin was wolfish. "I have plenty of money to spend on a girl like you."

Amanda clicked to Pal, turning her nose up at the man and trotting off as Theo's horse fell into step, and they left the rowdy town behind.

Teddy was seething as they rode out onto the open prairie. He would dearly like to poke Alder in the nose for his comments, but the truth was there. Amanda was a lady, raised to a life of wealth and ease he couldn't begin to compete with. He was nothing but a lowly cowpoke. He couldn't offer Amanda pretty things, a fancy house, and servants to do her bidding, but he could offer her love.

"Are there people living out this way?" Amanda's voice pulled him back from his thoughts.

"Yes, Prim and Anderson have a big ranch on this side of town. Peri and Bear live out this way too."

"So Needful is a little bigger than it appears." Amanda smiled brightly, enjoying the comfortable ride. The sun was warm, but they weren't pressing the horses or hurrying, allowing her to see the land around her with fresh eyes.

Teddy pulled Pepper to a stop as they topped a rise, leaning on his saddle horn and looking over the land. "Down that way a few days' ride, you'll come to Mexico," he said. "Dan does a bit of trade down that way, but no one has done much since Raul's passing."

"That was Rosa's first husband, wasn't it?"

"Yes, it's a shame about what happened to him. He was a good man and a good friend. Dan was pretty broken up about it all. It's why he wanted to help Rosa and Christina, but she wouldn't take it."

"They seem to have put that behind them now,"

Amanda grinned. "He's a good man."

"He is," Teddy agreed. "I wouldn't have followed him out here if he wasn't the kind to look after his own."

"You fought in the war together."

"Dan was my captain. He had this idea of moving away from all the places we had already been, and we came with him. It was a good move."

"And you have no family left anywhere?" Amanda's blue eyes were soft and Teddy pushed Pepper closer.

"None to speak of."

"I think I'm going to like riding here," Amanda said, turning and smiling as Teddy leaned in for a kiss. "It's a beautiful land."

"Just wait until you see it in the springtime," Teddy enthused. "The fields are blue with bluebells and wildflowers you ain't never seen before cover the earth like a patchwork quilt."

Amanda reached over, taking her husband's hand as he waxed poetic. Perhaps he was a simple cowhand, but he obviously had the heart of a romantic. He had been kind to her, despite the rough start of their relationship, and had been making up for his mistake at her arrival.

"What more do you want in life, Theodore?"

Teddy studied Amanda's profile as she gazed out over the plains.

"All I want is a peaceful life, a few head of cattle, maybe a couple of kids, and a woman to love," he replied.

Amanda felt her heart do a little leap in her breast at Theo's words. She knew she wasn't the kind of wife a man like Theodore needed, but he was willing to give her a chance at love. That was enough for her, and she redoubled her commitment to learn to be a good wife.

Rosa could teach her to cook, Beth could teach her to sew, and in time, she knew she would fit in as a bride of Needful. "That sounds like a beautiful dream," she said, still gazing at the grasslands below.

"Sometimes, if we wish hard enough," Teddy said, his words soft as a baby's breath, "dreams come true."

Amanda squeezed the rough hand that held hers and then turned her mount back toward town.

Chapter 14

Teddy woke to an empty bed, startled by Amanda's absence. Quickly donning his clothes for the day, he headed downstairs to see if she might have gone for an early breakfast or to visit Olive.

"She's not here," Shililiah said with a smile. "She asked Olive if there was somewhere she could get a bath."

Teddy looked down at his slightly wrinkled Sunday best and grimaced. He had washed well in the basin upstairs, but he was probably due for a good scrubbing himself.

"Thanks, Shi," he offered with a grin. "Could I get some coffee?"

The boarding house only served breakfast on Sunday and kept a big pot of stew simmering for men who needed supper. The men would bring lunch pails that were filled for a nickel. Otherwise, they had to fend for themselves.

"Have a seat," Shi smiled. "I'll bring your breakfast."

"Just coffee," Teddy corrected. "I'll wait for Amanda for breakfast."

"She had toast with tea already," Shi smiled again, her eyes twinkling with delight. "You might as well eat before we close the kitchen. It's Sunday, and we all have plenty to do." The young woman leaned over, giving him a wink. "Olive made up a big picnic for the family and packed one special for you and Amanda as well."

"That was very kind." Teddy was surprised by all the fuss, but perhaps she wanted to make sure that Amanda felt welcome here. "I'll thank her when I see her."

***

Amanda was loathe to get out of the oversized soaking tub that Olive and the other women of the Hampton household used. She really should have asked for a bath last night, but she was tired after her ride and was enjoying Theodore's company so much.

"You're going to turn into a prune if you stay in there much longer," Olive teased. "I have your dress all ready for you."

"Olive, you didn't need to do that." Amanda

rose from the water, wrapping herself in a towel. "It would have been fine."

"Nonsense," Olive insisted. "It's a beautiful dress, and you shouldn't have to go to church all wrinkled like that."

Amanda looked up, her eyes full of appreciation. "Thank you for everything."

"You're welcome. Now you'd best get dressed and ready. I'll be back in a minute to help you with the things."

Amanda dried herself then shimmied into her undergarments, slipping the corset over her silk chamise She would feel proud walking to church on her husband's arm.

"Here, now duck your head and I'll slip this lovely piece of work over your head." Olive walked in, carrying the dark rose-colored dress. "I even got the lace to settle at your throat."

In no time, Amanda was properly dressed, and Olive helped her pile her hair up in a simple knot. "Teddy's going to be tickled to see you."

Amanda grinned, checking her appearance in the mirror and heading to the dining room where Shi had informed her Teddy was having his breakfast.

Teddy stood to his feet as Amanda entered the room. She looked like a painted picture, and he hurried to offer her a chair.

"That color suits you," Teddy grinned. "Why I'll be escorting the prettiest girl in town to church this morning."

Amanda felt her cheeks heat but smiled with delight. It wasn't the first time a man had complimented her, but for some reason, Theo's words meant more than all the compliments she had received before.

"Do you want some breakfast?" Teddy took his seat, indicating the plate of bacon, eggs, and pancakes.

"No, I'll just have tea."

Teddy turned to summon one of the Hampton women, but Ellen was already delivering a fresh cup.

"I'll see you in church," she grinned, walking to the door and turning the closed sign around.

"I guess we have the place to ourselves," Teddy grinned. "I don't think I've ever seen the place so empty."

"It's rather romantic," Amanda looked up, meeting his eyes. "We have the place all to ourselves."

Teddy half stood leaning across the table and kissing her on the lips, laughing at the soft blush that graced her cheeks.

"We might as well take advantage of the opportunity," he said with a wink.

Amanda laughed, feeling relaxed and content. She was with someone she liked and felt that in time she might even love. The bath had refreshed her, and she felt pretty in her neatly pressed gown.

Teddy finished his breakfast and then stood, offering Amanda his arm. "I'll just go brush my teeth, and then we can head over to the church. Pastor plays some fine music before the service starts."

Amanda dabbed her lips on a napkin, placing it next to her plate as she rose and took Theodore's arm. She was suddenly looking forward to the service and seeing her new neighbors. After a good night's sleep, a hot bath, a good meal, and the encouragement of her friends, she felt like she could handle life in this cow town in Texas.

Even here in Needful, the women would be wearing their nicest dresses and Shi had said Olive planned a picnic for them all. It looked like a bright and beautiful day lay before them.

"What about the dishes?" Amanda asked, turning to look over her shoulder.

"I'll get them," young Felicity, Ellen and Joe's daughter, said slipping from the kitchen. "Mother asked me to check on you while she gets ready for church." The dark-haired girl smiled, admiring Amanda's dress.

"You look very lovely," Amanda smiled. "Thank you for your help."

Felicity looked down at her simple blue dress and pinafore but smiled at the compliment. One day she hoped she would have pretty dresses to wear once she was old enough to pin her hair up. Then the boys in school wouldn't pull her pigtails and call her skinny.

Teddy beamed as he escorted Amanda out of the dining room and toward their room. He was the luckiest man in Needful and would escort the most beautiful woman in town to church. Maybe, she wasn't used to simple living or ranch life, but he liked the way she smiled at him today.

***

"What are they doing?" Amanda asked, stopping on the boardwalk to stare as several burly men carried a battered piano into the church.

"The preacher made a deal with the saloon

keeper, that he'll play tunes every Saturday night at the saloon if he can have the piano on Sunday, and the bar is closed until after services." Teddy chuckled at the expression on his wife's face. Amada wasn't the first to be shocked by the unorthodox plan.

"You're kidding?"

"Nope," Teddy patted her hand, moving them toward the church where the first plinking notes of a tune began to rise.

Together the young couple greeted new neighbors and old acquaintances before taking a seat on one of the hard benches lining each side of the church.

Amanda grinned, her toe tapping to the raucous notes of a hymn played in a bold new way.

"I told ya," Teddy chuckled.

Soon, the music turned to singing and then the congregation settled in to silence for the reading of the word. The pastor's message was clear, concise, and to the point, which seemed to make a few of the men who had hauled the piano inside squirm on their hard seat.

The pastor had such conviction and spoke with such authority, that Amanda was entirely unprepared for the final words of the message and hesitated a moment before rising to sing a last song.

"It certainly is a lively church," she observed as she and Theo left the church, stopping to chat with friends along the way.

"Here's your basket," Olive said, walking up to Teddy and handing him a large basket before handing over an old quilt to Amanda. "You'd best find yourself a nice place to eat and get settled before the good ones are all gone." She turned, gazing out across the open grass and few shady spots around the church. "It seems a bunch of other folks had the same idea as we did."

Amanda laughed, watching as Olive hurried back to Orville, waving the family toward a tall old tree.

"Where would you like to sit?" Teddy asked. "There's a spot there by the woods if that suits you."

"That looks lovely," Amanda smiled.

They had only gone a few yards when a rough voice accosted them.

"Now isn't that sweet," Mr. Alder stepped out of the shade of the church building. "Why Teddy, I do think you've got yourself the prettiest girl in town." The older man's eyes raked Amanda with approval, but she ignored him. She had ignored rude men in her life, and this small man would not upset her.

"Now, darlin' if you get tired of trying to live rough with this cowpoke, you know you can always come to me. I've got a nice place above the saloon and enough money to buy you all the fancy dresses you want. Why I don't even care if you've been taken by young Teddy here, I like women with a few miles on them."

Teddy's fist connected with Alder's nose in a sickening crunch before Amanda had time to let loose with a scathing remark.

"Why you oaf, you hit me," the bartender grumbled. "I was just havin' some fun."

Teddy pulled back his fist again, but a steel grip wound around his wrist, arresting his momentum.

"Amanda, you'd best come with me," A woman's voice whispered in her ear as she gaped in horror at her husband's bloody fist and the saloon owner's gushing nose.

"Theodore," Pastor Barton spoke, his voice a sharp bark as he held to Teddy's arm. "I'd like a word with you."

Amanda watched as several men came to attend to the saloon owner while her husband was pulled away by the preacher.

"Why did he do that?" She asked, turning toward Beth, who now held both quilt and basket in her hands. "The man wasn't worth it."

"Come sit down and we'll talk," Beth said. "I've already started on your first dress," she added, hoping to distract Amanda from the unpleasantness of a moment ago.

Amanda followed the preacher's wife to a spot near the trees that she and Theodore had been headed to. Soon she was sitting on the blanket sipping cold tea and wondering when Teddy would return.

***

"I'm afraid that was not a very wise thing for Teddy to do," Beth said. "I know he feels like he isn't good enough for you, but he'll get over that in time."

"He isn't good enough for me?" Amanda turned wide eyes on the pastor's wife.

"Of course," Beth smoothed her skirts then met Amanda's eyes. "Teddy is a simple man. He's carrying a lot of weight and leftover hurt from the war, and now, he's married himself a real lady. I'm sure he feels like he's the luckiest and most undeserving man in town."

"But why? I'm useless as a wife. I can't cook or clean. I had to stop helping Rosa with the dishes because my hands were so raw." Amanda lifted her gloved hands in supplication.

Beth settled her hands over Amanda's. "Those things you can learn," she said. "But Teddy knows he'll never be a gentleman. He's just a cowboy who married a lady."

Amanda shook her head. "He shouldn't have hit that man. I know the creature was being odious, but he wasn't worth our time."

"Teddy was defending your honor."

"My honor doesn't need defending," Amanda sighed. "I've had all sorts of insults tossed at me over the years in the city. Some men are simply rude. The best thing to do is to ignore them."

Beth smiled. "We know that, but men sometimes don't see it that way." The young woman leaned in closer to Amanda and grinned. "To be honest, I think Mr. Alder deserved it. He's been trying to filch on his agreement with Brandon. The man thinks that because he takes money from poor, hard-working miners, farmers, and cowhands, he's a big deal. Maybe this will bring him down a peg."

Amanda gaped at Beth then broke out with a laugh. It had been silly of Teddy to do what he did, but it was also sweet in a misguided sort of way.

***

"Now preacher," Teddy started as they walked into the church. "Don't start lecturing me on turning the other cheek and the like. Alder shouldn't have said such a thing to my wife."

"No, I don't suppose he should have, but do you think he deserved a punch in the nose?"

Teddy scuffed his foot on the plank floor, just inside the church door. "It seemed like the thing to do at the time."

Brandon chuckled. "I'm sure you aren't the first man to think that. I believe Alder is looking for attention is all. Things are quieting down here in Needful, and folks don't look so kindly on his presence as they used to."

"He still has plenty of business, though."

"That's true, but don't let him get under your skin. He isn't worth it."

"That's what Amanda said as well."

"She's a smart woman."

"And too good for me," the words leapt from Teddy's mouth so fast he couldn't recall them.

"So that's the problem," Brandon nodded. "I thought there might be more to your reaction to Alder. Teddy," Brandon placed a hand on Theodore's shoulder. "That girl chose you. Don't shame her by second guessing her choice."

Teddy stood, shrugging off the preacher's hand. "But she's a fine lady, and I'm just a cowhand."

"That's not true." Brandon stood, meeting Teddy's hot gaze. "You're far more than a cowhand. You're a good friend, loyal, hard-working, and true. I know Dan trusts you, not only with his cattle but with his life."

Teddy dropped his gaze, his mind racing back to the war and his foolish acts of what Dan called bravery. "I look out for them I care for."

"And that is why Amanda will grow to love you. Let her see the man inside. Don't hide who you are, worrying about what you can or can't give that girl. Maybe she is a fine lady, but she has made her choice, and with love, understanding, and care, she'll find her way as your wife. The two of you stood before me last week exchanging your vows. I didn't see any hesitation in her words."

"You really think so?" Teddy looked up, meeting the preacher's gaze once more.

"Teddy, a woman doesn't just want things, she wants love. You could give her the world, but if you couldn't love her, she would always be lacking."

"I don't know, Preacher. She's always had everything she wanted. How will she adjust to life as my wife?"

"Make her a part of that life," Brandon said. "Share everything with her, your job, your finances, and your worries. Build a partnership where she's as much a part of your world as the very breath you breathe."

Teddy scratched the back of his neck. "You really think it will make a difference?"

"I know it will."

"I reckon I'd better join my wife." Teddy grinned. "She's expecting a picnic." Teddy turned, walking out the door pondering the preacher's words.

Chapter 15

"Theo?" Amanda asked as her husband returned, slumping to the blanket she had spread in the shade of the trees. "Do you want to go home?"

"No," Teddy shrugged, dropping to the blanket, his head hanging. "I promised you a picnic."

Amanda looked at her dejected spouse, wondering what she should do. Reaching out, she pulled his hat from his head, placing it next to her knee. "Oh, your hand," she said, pointing at his battered knuckles. "Let me see."

Teddy reached out his hand, flinching as Amanda wrapped her handkerchief around it, tying it off with gentle fingers.

"Why did you do it?" Amanda asked, waiting until Theo met her gaze. "It wasn't worth it."

Teddy shook his head, shame making his face flush. "He shouldn't have said what he did," he tried, hoping to justify his actions.

"No, but what he says shouldn't determine your behavior."

Teddy offered Amanda a half-grin in acknowledgment of her words. "It's true," he finally spoke. "You should have married a man who could give you all the nice things you're used to. A nice house, servants, fancy clothes." He lifted the soft ruffle around her skirt as sorrow and shame washed over him.

"If that was all I wanted, I could have stayed home. My step-father would have found an appropriate man for me to marry, someone who would bring more wealth to the family through land, investment, or assets. I didn't want that."

"But I'm just a cowhand," Teddy objected. "I have a tiny house, and you have to learn to do all the things you always had done for you. It doesn't seem fair."

Amanda grinned, reaching for the basket and placing the food on the blanket. "Theodore, I chose you. You may not have all of the things I grew up with, but you're honest and true. That is what I need more than anything else. When I left home…" Amanda paused, handing Theo a plate. "It wasn't just that I didn't like my step-father. I thought he was a rude and greedy man, but it was more than that."

Teddy took the plate Amanda offered, meeting her eyes as curiosity got the best of him. "Did he behave inappropriately?"

"No," Amanda shook her head. "At one point, I went into town to meet a friend for tea. While we were out, I saw my stepfather with another woman." Amanda's cheeks flushed as she continued. "She did not appear to be a woman of good repute."

"And that's why you left."

"I tried to speak to my mother, but she wouldn't listen. She said that her new husband was a good man and that he would never do anything to cause her pain. When I tried to argue, she told me that if I was going to spread lies about the man she loved that I should leave."

Teddy's eyes widened at the words, and he reached for Amanda's hand, giving it a soft squeeze. "I'm sorry."

"Perhaps you aren't rich and you don't have all the fancy things I grew up with," Amanda continued. "But you are honest. When you told me you would provide for and protect me, I knew it was true."

Teddy's lips twitched into a sad smile. "And love," he said. "I'm already half in love with you, and I want that to grow."

Amanda smiled, dropping her eyes shyly. "I like you too," she admitted, her heart fluttering. "I look forward to learning to love you more each day."

Amanda finished filling her plate and picked up a fork, taking a delicate bite of the delicious meal prepared for them. She still wasn't happy about Teddy's behavior, but she could understand how he felt. It wasn't fair that a good man like Theodore had to scrape for everything he had, while men like Mr. Alder grew fat and rich profiting from the vices of other men.

Together they ate in companionable silence, finishing the meal as the sun grew high.

"How about a stroll to the stream?" Teddy asked, handing his plate back to Amanda, who packed it carefully into the basket. "It's pretty this time of year. Shallow, but pretty."

"I think I'd like that," Amanda grinned. "Then, we can take this back to the Hampton House, settle up, and head home."

The way Amanda said home filled Teddy with joy, hope, and cheer. After so long with nowhere to truly call home, he felt that anywhere with the beautiful woman who had become his wife was truly home.

"It is pretty here," Amanda said a few minutes

later as she walked arm in arm with Theodore under the shade of twisted cottonwoods growing along the stream.

"It's cool and quiet," Teddy agreed. "I always like comin' along here on a Sunday. Back home, we had a stream that flowed through the property."

"You never told me where you were from," Amanda said.

"Kentucky," Teddy said, still walking. "It was a long time ago, and there's nothing there now. My folks died while I was away fightin'."

"I'm sorry."

Teddy turned, looking down into blue eyes filled with compassion. "I was angry a long time," he said. "It was a bad time, but I'm learning that God has a plan for each of us. A path that's different than anyone else's."

Amanda stopped, turning to look up into Theo's face, hidden in shadow by his new wide-brimmed hat. Reaching out, she pulled the hat from his head, letting it dangle from her fingertips as she smiled up at him.

Teddy touched Amanda's face, brushing her cheek with a gentle hand. "You're sure pretty," he drawled.

Amanda blushed, liking the feel of Theo's hand on her face. "Thank you," she blushed.

Teddy leaned in, brushing Amanda's lips with his. Somewhere between the moment he had punched the saloon owner in the nose, and now, he realized he already loved his little wife. He didn't care if she ever learned to cook, clean, or do the wash. She was exactly what he needed.

***

"You come to see us anytime you want to now," Olive said as Teddy and Amanda prepared to depart. "You're welcome to pop in for tea and a visit whenever you can."

"I will," Amanda promised, squeezing the older woman's hand. "Now that I have a horse to ride and a proper saddle, I can come to town anytime I need to."

Teddy raised an eyebrow but didn't say anything. He wanted Amanda to feel free to come and go as she pleased, but he didn't like the idea of her traveling to town alone.

"We'll see ya next week," he offered, waving at the Hampton's. "We have a busy week ahead."

Amanda waved, giving her friends a backward glance, as Teddy helped her up onto Pal's back. "I'll have to have you come visit as well," she called, her eyes falling on Ellen. "As soon as I learn how to make a pot of tea."

A soft titter of laughter followed the couple down the street toward the ranch.

"I can't believe you said that," Teddy grinned.

"Why not?" Amanda smiled at her husband. "Everyone knows I'm all but useless in the home-making department. That doesn't mean I can't learn. Besides, if I can't learn to laugh at myself, I'll make life miserable for both of us."

Teddy reached across the space between them, taking her hand. "I knew there was a reason I liked you."

Amanda grinned, a wicked gleam entering her eyes as she released Theo's hand and urged Pal into a run. "Catch me if you can."

With a sharp laugh Teddy, kicked Pepper into a run to match Pal. His little wife did have pluck; it just took some time for her to show it.

Chapter 16

The sound of galloping hooves filled the evening as Teddy raced to keep up with Amanda. Her dark hair had come unpinned and flowed behind her, making him grin. He had never seen a woman ride like that, and it made his heart swell with pride as they thundered toward the ranch.

The girl was full of a spark that had remained hidden, but now flared into flame. If only he could love her well enough, perhaps some of that same heat would glow in her eyes for him. She was beautiful, smart, funny, and could ride like the wind.

Together they galloped over the hill, making the turn toward the ranch. Dark clouds crested the horizon to the east, as the sun slipped lower on the horizon, painting the sky a glowing blood-red in the wake of the oncoming storm. Mounds of black clouds were painted in steaks of pink and gold as the thunderheads broke in the distance.

Teddy pressed his hat tighter on his head as the wind kicked up dust, blowing it into a whirlwind of grit. "Amanda, make for the ranch," he shouted over the gusting wind. "A storm's coming."

Amanda nodded as a flash of lightning sizzled on the distant hills, shattering the sky with a roar.

Leaning over Pal's neck, Amanda urged the horse to quicken the pace, hoping to outrun the sheet of rain sweeping toward them in a curtain of gray.

Pepper stretched out, ears flat along his neck as he felt his rider's desperation, driving past, Pal.

Teddy looked back over his shoulder as Amanda gave the little palomino her head, hoping they would make the safety of the ranch before the storm reached them.

Another lightning strike split the sky as wind flattened the long grass along the prairie, and Amanda screamed, watching as Pepper stumbled, toppling forward, and taking Teddy with him.

Teddy felt himself tumbling as Pepper fell, the tall pinto flipping over, a flailing hoof connecting with Teddy's temple as the world crashed into blackness.

Amanda dragged in on the reins, clinging to the saddle as Pal slid to a stop, twisting and pivoting on hindquarters of steel. "Teddy!" she screamed over the sound of the approaching storm. Throwing herself from the saddle as Pepper staggered to his feet with a shake of his head, Amanda hurried to her husband's side. "Teddy," she called again, running her hands over his body where he lay in the dust of the trail.

Amanda lifted Teddy's shoulders, trying to determine if he had any broken bones, but none were apparent. "Please wake up, Theo," she pleaded. Staring into his face and seeing the small trickle of blood on his head, as the wind howled around her. Gently, easing Theo back to the ground, Amanda hurried to the horses where they stood nervously twitching at the blast of cold wind.

"Easy girl," Amanda soothed, grasping Pal's reins and pulling the animal close.

"You have to help Pal," she said as the wind tugged at her skirts, blowing dust into her tear-filled eyes. Quickly she gathered Pepper's reins and tied them then moved closer to Theo.

The wind swirled dust into a pillar of cloud as Amanda took Pal's left rein in her right hand, then bent, lifting Pal's near front leg and tugging on the bridle, making the horse touch nose to shoulder until she overbalanced and sagged to the ground. Slipping the rein into her mouth to hold it taut, Amanda grabbed Teddy under the arms and dragged his limp form over the saddle. Heaving and breathless, she slipped a leg over the horse's haunches, grasped the front of the saddle and let the horse lurch to her feet.

"Home," she called to Pal, aiming the pretty pony toward the ranch.

Pal's ears twitched as Amanda's hands clutched the saddle bows holding Theo in place and urged the horse forward as the leading edge of the storm began to splatter the ground with huge icy drops of rain.

"Please, God, let him be alright," Amanda pleaded as tears mingled with the first spattering of icy raindrops and urging her horse for more speed.

Glancing behind her, Amanda sighed as Pepper galloped along in her wake, apparently uninjured by his fall.

"Help!" Amanda shouted as the ranch came into view. "Help!" She cried again as a flash of lightning crackled, raising the hair on her neck. Thunder boomed overhead and the heavens opened.

***

"Daniel, you hear that?"

"What's that, Rosa?" Dan looked from the table where he had been going over a ledger.

"I hear something," Rosa turned from the stove

where she had settled the coffee pot, "someone shouting."

Dan jumped to his feet as a crack of thunder shook the sturdy house and raced to the front door, even as Pal and Pepper stumbled into the yard.

"Amanda!" Dan shouted over the deluge, blinking to see what she was doing on her own. "What's wrong?" Dan raised a hand, trying to ward off the driving rain.

"Help," the word came out a strangled cry, swept away by the wind and rain.

"What's going on?" Dozer staggered from the barn, pushing toward the two horses as the rain soaked him in an instant.

"Teddy," Amanda sobbed, still holding her husband on the saddle before her. "Pepper fell."

Strong hands reached up, pulling Teddy from the horse's back as Dan reached for Amanda, who collapsed into his arms, fear and exhaustion turning her muscles to liquid.

Dozer carried Teddy into the house, placing him on the settee in the lounge as Dan placed a soaked Amanda in a chair,a looking to Rosa for help.

"What happened?" he asked, walking to Teddy when Rosa hurried to his side.

"We were trying to outrun the storm," Amanda said, her voice shaking as she began to shiver. "Theo looked back, and Pepper stumbled, taking them both down. Please tell me he isn't dead," she added with a sniff.

"He is not dead," Rosa declared, walking to Amanda and grasping her hand. "Daniel, get him out of those wet clothes. Amanda, come with me, you must change."

"But, Theo."

"He lives, we can do nothing but wait."

Amanda stood, legs shaking and followed Rosa to another room where she quickly stripped out of her soaked dress and into one of Rosa's simple but comfortable ones. "Do you think he will be all right?" she asked.

"We will pray," Rosa said, her dark eyes filled with conviction. "Teddy will be fine."

"He's still out," Dan said, looking up as the women returned. "Dozer took the horses," he added, looking at Amanda. "You did good getting here."

"I didn't know what else to do," Amanda admitted. "I don't know where I found the strength."

Rosa squeezed her hand. "From your heart," she said softly, releasing Amanda's hand and lifting a blanket from a chair to lay it over Teddy. "I make tea."

Rosa was gone, turning on her heel and heading for the kitchen as Amanda sat on the chair, watching Teddy, a wave of nervous exhaustion making her sag.

"He'll be all right," Dan said, walking to Amanda and offering her another blanket. "Teddy's been through far worse."

Amanda looked up, her blue eyes sad. "When?"

"In the war," Dan said, turning to study his friend. "He got pinned down in enemy territory, doing reconnaissance. Haven't you ever wondered about the scar on his leg?"

Amanda blushed. She had never questioned Theo about his previous injuries, assuming they were from run-ins with cantankerous cows. "No."

"Teddy was never afraid to do what needed doing. He was young and small and could slip in and out of camp unseen. This time, someone saw him, and he took a bullet to his calf. He made it back, but he'd lost a lot of blood. It was weeks before he could walk properly again."

Amanda turned her eyes full of affection and pride for the man she had married. "He was brave."

"Always. Even going against orders when it was the right thing to do."

"He disobeyed you?"

"No, not me. I wouldn't have put him in that position, but some officers weren't near as good as they thought they were. One man captured a group of Rebs and chained them all, even the black serving men with them. Teddy talked until he was blue in the face about releasing them, but the officer wouldn't listen. That night, Theodore Lewis walked out to the captives and released the slaves. He was whipped for it, but he never said a word in his defense."

Amanda stood, walking to the settee and slipping to the floor next to Theo, taking his hand in hers. "He was worried that he wasn't good enough for me," she said, studying his face. "But, he's exactly what I needed."

Dan smiled, nodding once as he slipped out of the room, leaving Amanda and Teddy alone.

"Please be all right," Amanda pleaded, tears filling her eyes once more. "Don't you know I love you already?"

Teddy's eyes fluttered open as a gray light

stabbed his vision. "Amanda," he called, his heart thudding with fear.

"I'm here," Amanda said, squeezing his hand. "We're home."

"Home? How?"

"Your wife brought you in," Dan said, walking in with a tray of tea in his hands, Rosa on his heels, carrying Christina on a hip.

"She is a hero," Rosa said.

"Help me up," Teddy said, his head spinning as he tried to pull himself upright.

Dan placed the tea things on the table by the settee and moved to help Teddy sit upright. "Take it easy," he said. "You had a nasty bump on the head."

Amanda took the hand Dan offered and rose, taking the seat next to Teddy, who clutched the blanket to his chest.

"What happened to my clothes?"

"You were wet," Rosa shrugged.

"Dan took them," Amanda grinned, taking a cup and adding cream and sugar, then lifting it to Theo. "Drink this, it will help."

Teddy tried to glare at her, but his pounding head prevented it, and he ended up taking a sip of the sweet, hot tea.

"Pepper, fell," Amanda said softly as she urged Teddy to take another sip of the tea. "I got you on Pal and came to the ranch."

"Pepper?"

"He's alright," Dan said. "He followed Amanda and Pal home. Dozer put both horses in the barn."

A crash of thunder made Amanda jump, and she quickly placed the cup and saucer back on the tray.

"Bad storm?" Teddy asked, pulling an arm from under the blanket and wrapping it protectively around his wife. "I remember. We were trying to get home before we got caught in it. It whipped up out of nowhere."

"You're safe now," Amanda smiled, feeling some of the tension ebbing from weary shoulders. "We made it home."

"How?" Teddy reached up, touching the dried blood on his head.

"I pulled Pal, down so I could drag you onto the saddle," Amanda admitted. "I think it was the fright that gave me the strength. It all happened so fast. All I knew was that I had to get us to the ranch."

Dan walked back into the room, carrying a nightshirt. "This will have to do for now," the ranch owner grinned. "Once the rain lets up, you two can head back to your place or Rosa can make up the spare room for you."

Amanda turned, looking out the window at the pouring rain. "I hope it eases soon." She looked at Theo, taking his hand in hers. "I think I'd like to be in our own home tonight."

Teddy felt his heart swell. His sweet little Amanda, the young woman who didn't seem to know how to do much of anything, had probably saved his life. He could see the affection shining in her eyes and his fingers tightened in hers.

"Thanks, Dan." Teddy reached for the nightshirt, slipping his hand from Amanda's and pulling it over his head. It was far too wide in the shoulders, but it would do for now.

"Any time," Dan grinned, turning on his heel as he wrapped an arm around Rosa, leading her to the kitchen and leaving Teddy and Amanda alone once more.

"How'd you know to get Pal to lie down?" Teddy asked, sliding the nightshirt over his knees. "I don't think I would have thought of that."

"It just came to me," Amanda admitted, looking at him closely. "I had to do something. I couldn't lose you." She sniffled, feeling all of the adrenaline ebbing away. "I don't know what I'd do if I lost you, Theodore."

Teddy wrapped his arm around Amanda again, pulling her close. "I'm not going anywhere, love," he said, pressing a kiss to her brow. "You're stuck with me now."

A nervous giggle escaped Amanda's lips and she dabbed at her nose. "That suits me fine."

The couple sat there snuggled close on the settee for a while longer, quietly waiting for the storm to pass. They had already been through a few trials, and it had brought them closer. Perhaps in time, they would truly be as one.

"I think the rain is passing." Teddy's voice was soft. "Do you want to try to go home?"

"Yes," Amanda stirred, lifting her head from his shoulder and stifling a yawn. "I think I'm looking forward to a hot bath and my own bed."

Teddy grinned. "You know you'll have to heat the water yourself?"

"I know," Amanda turned her blue eyes meeting his. "I'll learn," she assured. "Maybe it will take me a while, but I'll get there in the end."

Teddy kissed her forehead, sweetly. "You're a much stronger woman than anyone might think."

***

"Theo, I can do this myself," Amanda growled, hefting a bucket from the fireplace. "I have decided that I want a cookstove, though, just something small. I can start by learning to make tea and coffee."

"Yes, ma'am," Teddy teased, his grin widening. His head still hurt slightly but watching his determined little wife heating water for their new tub lifted his spirits.

"You can bathe first," Amanda continued, pouring the water into the tub and heading for the rain barrel by the door.

"Me? I just washed last night?"

"Yes, but you are injured, and we were both soaked to the skin. We don't want to catch a chill."

Teddy bit his lip, repressing a laugh. Amanda seemed to have found her confidence, and it filled him with pride. Despite her evident weariness after the hard ride and drama of earlier, she was stubbornly determined to have a hot bath before bed.

Taking a seat, Teddy stripped off his boots, pulling the nightshirt over his head and wrapping it around his middle.

"It's ready," Amanda smiled. She had poured another bucket of hot water into the tub, topping it up with some of the cold water from the rain barrel. "You go on."

Teddy walked to the tub, testing the water with his toe. "It's hot."

"It's supposed to be hot," Amanda's retort was short. "I'll get soap."

Teddy slipped into the tub, sighing as the hot water lapped over his hips. His little wife had been right. This was just what he needed.

Amanda blushed prettily as she walked back to the tub, a washrag and bar of soap in her hand. She had never honestly looked at her husband this way, and her eyes strayed to the puckered scar in his right calf as she handed him the items.

"This smells like flowers," Teddy grumbled.

"It's all I have," Amanda sigh, brushing a lock of tangled hair from her eyes. "If you want something else, you'll have to put it on the shopping list."

Teddy lathered up the cloth and gingerly

washed the blood from his brow, flinching as the hot water burned.

"Here, let me." Amanda's soft hands took the cloth, her eyes colliding with Theo's as a wicked grin spread across his face. "Theo!" she screeched as Teddy pulled her into the tub with him.

Epilogue

"I need to be going," Amanda said, rising and donning her gloves. "Theo finally stopped fussing about me riding to town alone, but he doesn't like me getting home too late."

"I'm glad you came," Olive said.

"Me too," Ellen grinned.

Over the past two months, the ladies had grown closer, and Amanda felt like she had true friends in Needful. She had even attended a sewing circle a few times, though her stitches were abysmal.

"It does get dark rather early now that the days are growing shorter again." Amanda looked around her, checking that she hadn't forgotten anything.

"And cooler, thank the Lord," Ellen grinned.

Amanda's smile was bright. "Yes, the Texas heat is something to contend with. I'll see you all on Sunday."

The sound of the stage arriving made all three women start as Amanda headed for the door.

"It's late for the stage," Olive said, a flicker of worry flashing in her eyes as she pushed to her feet and following Amanda to the door.

"Is that the stage?" Orville hustled out of the back of the house, scowling at the interruption.

"It seems to be," Olive replied.

Amanda stepped out onto the front porch, her eyes taking in the same stage she had arrived in only two short months ago.

"Special delivery," the driver called down with a grin, as an older gentleman began to climb down from the seat on the top of the coach.

"We're here," the man said, shuffling to the door of the stage. "You can finally come out."

Amanda turned, giving Olive a questioning glance, but the older woman simply shrugged.

"Is either of you ladies Olive Hampton or Peri?" the man asked, his gnarled hand falling on the handle of the stage door.

"I'm Olive Hampton."

"I'm Phineas Fortuna," the man said, pulling the door open, "and these are my daughters, come to be mail-order brides."

Olive's mouth fell open as a tall, austere looking woman of nearly thirty stepped onto the boardwalk, her pinched mouth and hard eyes taking in the town with a critical glance.

"This is Adele, my oldest."

"Ma'am." The young woman curtsied slightly, straightening a little unsteadily. Her dark eyes were keen, but the severe pull of her tight bun did nothing to soften the lines of her angular face.

"This one is Heidi," Mr. Fortuna spoke, handing a mousy looking girl from the coach. Her dark eyes were large and startled, looking as she gazed around her absently, trying to tuck an untidy strand of brown hair into the loose bun at the back of her head.

"Hello," she said, blinking into the light. "Is this Texas?"

Olive shot a glance toward Amanda but greeted the girl warmly.

"Olga, you're next," the old man's voice was harsh as he beckoned another girl, this one blonde and plump, from the stage. "Stop messing with your dress," he barked. "No one cares what you look like after a long ride."

"But Papa," Olga said, smoothing her fashionable, but hideous pea green dress, "what if my new husband sees me. I want to make a good impression."

Phineas rolled his eyes but took his daughter by the hand, helping her down the step shaking his head as he took in the horrid color of her dress, which clashed severely with her fair complexion and pale eyes.

"Fanny. Fanny!" the man shouted. "We're here."

"Oh," a disembodied voice echoed from the shadowy depths of the stage. "Take these."

A small hamper appeared, followed by a stack of bound books.

"I don't want that beast," Mr. Fortuna said as the hamper began to hiss and growl. "You know it hates everyone, but you."

A slip of a girl finally immerged from the darkness within, her light brown hair neatly tucked into a knitted snood. "Papa, you know that Midas is a dear and an excellent mouser to boot. Please don't be rude."

Olive covered her mouth with her hand, too flabbergasted to speak.

"I didn't expect you tonight?" Orville came

around the side of the boarding house, driving a fresh team of stage horses. Rather late, you know."

"I'll be staying the night," the driver called down, reaching for a trunk strapped to the coach.

"Oh, do be careful!" the third daughter called. "My clothing is in there and you wouldn't want to damage anything. I've copied all of the latest fashions from Paris."

Phineas Fortuna ran a hand over his face, he looked weary and at his wit's end.

"Well, here they are," he sighed, looking at Olive. "What do you want to do with them?"

Olive gaped, looking at the young women lined up outside her door as Orville turned his snorting team back toward the livery stable.

"Amanda?" Teddy's voice echoed onto the porch as Orville turned his team around, and the stage driver handed down boxes, bags, and trunks.

"I'm here, Theo," Amanda grinned. "You didn't have to come for me. I was on my way home."

Teddy stepped down from his horse, hitching him to the rail as the stage driver clicked to his tired team, turning them in the street. "Dan sent me for some things, so I thought we could ride home together." The young man gazed at the group of people standing awkwardly on the boardwalk. "Who are these folks?"

"These are the Fortunas," Amanda grinned, casting her eyes between the girls and Olive. "They're the new brides of Needful."

Olive shook herself, sprinting into action and hustling the family into the house. There was work to be done. "I'll see you in church," she called, following the girls inside. "Mr. Fortuna, I'll show you all to your rooms, my boys will be out to collect the bags."

Teddy rubbed the back of his neck as the family of five disappeared into the Hampton House. "Who was that man with the girls?"

"That's their father," Amanda tittered, finding the situation suddenly funny. "It appears that he feels they all need husbands." She looked up, smoothing the skirt of her simple blue and green plaid dress.

Teddy wrapped an arm around Amanda, pulling her tight. "I'm sure relieved that I met you before they arrived, he grinned. Not one of them girls can hold a candle to you."

Amanda snuggled into Teddy's warm embrace. She liked it when he talked sweet. "You were mighty lucky," she grinned. "After all, it isn't every day a young woman arrives in Needful and falls into your arms."

Teddy grinned, his ears flushing pink. "You know I love you, right?"

"I do," Amanda said, gazing into his bright eyes. "I love you too, but I never get tired of hearing you say it."

"I hope I show it to," Teddy grinned.

Amanda blushed, then smoothed Theo's shirt. "You have been trying hard," she admitted. "You even made me that lovely press for my clothing."

Teddy peered around him and then dropped his lips to hers. "Let's go home, wife," he grinned, taking her work-roughened hand in his. "I'd take you to supper at the boarding house, but I think the Hamptons will have their hands full for quite a while."

Amanda's bright laugh echoed down the street as together, she and Theodore raced out of Needful, full of love, hope, and determination to find their own way.

The End

Books In This Series

Brides of Needful, Texas
Mail-order Brides are just what Needful, Texas needs the most and Olive Hampton is determined to see the town tamed, one woman at a time.

Join her adventures in the burgeoning cowtown and see if everything goes to plan.

Daliah

Orphan Daliah Owens has been working for the Smithfield bank for two years without a problem at least until the new manager arrives and her drawer suddenly comes up short. Dismissed from her job and disgraced by a crime she didn't commit, Daliah seeks a second chance with an elderly couple heading to Texas on a wagon train. Facing the hardships of the trail with bravery, compassion, and faith Daliah quickly endears herself to not only her employer but many of the other members of the band as well. Invaluable in her knowledge of herbs for healing and nutrition she is soon recognized as an indispensable helper to all.

Spencer Gaines, still bitter after the loss of his wife is a hard man to talk to, but his five-year-old son Chad, and greatest treasure is more trouble than he can handle. Determined to finally settle down near his brother in Texas Spencer signs on as a chief scout for the wagon train but his duties often lead him far afield leaving Chad to get into so many scrapes they could both well be dismissed.

Will a devastating accident leave Spencer empty and alone forever or will he not only learn to trust God but also give Daliah his heart?

Prim

The loss of her father has left Primrose Perkins in need of a way to provide not only for herself but also for her mother and sister. With a new and wonderful sense of freedom to discover who she can be, her decisions could be the answer to all of their troubles. Will she be able to find a way to ensure that her family will be cared for by answering an ad for a mail-order bride, or will deception lead her astray?

Needful Texas is a growing town with growing troubles. Rowdy cowhands, drunken parties, and wealthy ranchers who don't think they need to become a part of the community.

How can Prim, find a home and the help she needs

in a town with more men than is good for it?

Peri

Periwinkle Perkins is determined to become an independent woman. After the death of her father and departure of her sister Prim, Peri knows that she can't live off the generosity of her aunt forever. Tasked with caring for her invalid mother while her older sister tries to establish a new home for them as a mail-order bride, Peri sets out to find the money her recently deceased father has hidden. If she can only find Pa's stash Periwinkle can take her mother to Needful Texas to join her sister and set up a home of her own. Always a hopeless romantic before Peri now wishes only for the security of a steady income to provide for her mother, but will she find the funds she needs or be stranded while her sister seeks a man who is willing to accept a fully formed family? Desperate times called for desperate measure and Peri know she is up to the task.

Beth

Elizabeth Beechen only wishes to leave the pain and sorrow of loss behind and find a new life in Needful, Texas. Prepared to be a mail-order bride, she sets out on her journey only to find that the situation in the tiny town has changed and she needs to adjust quickly. Mustering a positive attitude and determined to love her new home, despite its growing pains, she finds friendship in the course of adversity.

Can she learn to trust God enough to believe that the man He has waiting for her won't suffer from the same vices her father did, leaving her alone and lonely for the rest of her life?

Ruth

Ruth Warthan is tired of her sedentary life. She longs for adventure, excitement, and most of all love, but her overly protective parents are content for her to stay with them forever, shunning even a hint of romance. Will an advertisement for a mail-order bride in faraway Texas be the answer to her prayers, or will she find that her parents were right, and she isn't suited for marriage or life outside their cloistered home?

Rosa

Another Needful Bride!

Rosa Rodriguez is independent for the first time in her life. She has a job she enjoys, and a way to provide for herself and her daughter. Surrounded by friends, she battles the sorrow, anger, and shame of the past, uncertain of what her future could bring.

Will her misconceptions, doubts, and lack of trust

steal her chance at love?

Dan Gaines has been focused on building his ranch, providing for his men, and caring for the town of Needful. As the reluctant mayor of the tiny cow town, he is determined to meet the needs of all who live there, but one particularly stubborn woman won't let him help. As his frustration turns to infatuation, his feelings of personal guilt over his friend's death keeps him from seeing what is right before his eyes. Will circumstances, misunderstandings, and danger separate him from the one who owns his heart?

Made in the USA
Coppell, TX
25 March 2022